HANNAH & THE WILD WOODS

Hannah &
the Wild Woods

Carol Anne Shaw

RONSDALE PRESS

HANNAH & THE WILD WOODS
Copyright © 2015 Carol Anne Shaw

RONSDALE PRESS
3350 West 21st Avenue, Vancouver, B.C., Canada V6S 1G7
www.ronsdalepress.com

Typesetting: Julie Cochrane, in Minion 12 pt on 16
Cover Art & Design: Nancy de Brouwer, Massive Graphic Design
Paper: Ancient Forest Friendly "Silva" (FSC)—100% post-consumer waste, totally chlorine-free and acid-free

Ronsdale Press wishes to thank the following for their support of its publishing program: the Canada Council for the Arts, the Government of Canada through the Canada Book Fund, the British Columbia Arts Council and the Province of British Columbia through the British Columbia Book Publishing Tax Credit program.

Library and Archives Canada Cataloguing in Publication

Shaw, Carol Anne, 1960–, author
  Hannah & the wild woods / Carol Anne Shaw.

Issued in print and electronic formats.
ISBN 978-1-55380-440-6 (paper)
ISBN 978-1-55380-441-3 (ebook) / ISBN 978-1-55380-442-0 (pdf)

  1. Tohoku Earthquake and Tsunami, Japan, 2011—Juvenile fiction.
I. Title. II. Title: Hannah and the wild woods.

PS8637.H383H8 2015   jC813'.6   C2015-902994-5   C2015-902995-3

At Ronsdale Press we are committed to protecting the environment. To this end we are working with Canopy and printers to phase out our use of paper produced from ancient forests. This book is one step towards that goal.

Printed in Canada by Marquis Printing, Quebec

for Peter and Kim

ACKNOWLEDGEMENTS

Hannah and the Wild Woods went through numerous drafts. I loved it, hated it, wanted to burn it, wanted to paper the walls with it, stared at it, threw it out, started again, and then finally stopped moaning and finished it. I guess some books are just like that. I ended up loving the story. I hope you do, too.

My heartfelt thanks to my writing group, FRANK: Kristine Paton, Cameron Bucknum, James Funfer, Kimberley Phillips, Selinde Krayenhoff and James Holland. You guys keep things real, and for that I am so grateful. Tim and Gillian Coy, thank you so much for opening up your delightful cottage on Gabriola for me to escape to from time to time. Your generosity and kindness is appreciated. Shawnigan House Coffee, your homemade chocolate is food of the Gods. Ron, Veronica and fellow Ronsdalians, thank you for all you do. You are all such pros, and I continue to learn much from all of you. Richard, thanks for reminding me of the *three stages of book writing*, especially when I was stuck in stage two. (Stage two: *I can't write and I hate everyone.*) Nick, thank you for being such a patient sounding board, and Trevor, that little heater rocks! Eddie (Shiny Bob), what would I do without my morning couch companion? There was never a better muse.

And finally, a huge thank you to all the young readers I have met visiting local schools and libraries in the past few years. When I feel my energy lag, it is your questions, gorgeous drawings and heartfelt letters that get me back in the game. You are the reason I write.

Prologue

THE GIRL SEES THE fleeing of the birds, then feels the fast rush of air. For a moment she cannot comprehend the surge of raging muddy water that crests the seawall and spills into the streets below.

The chaos is immediate. The world spins. There are screams, sounds of wood splitting, metal grating and, above everything, the deafening roar of rushing water.

From where the girl stands on the roof of the building, she can see in every direction, and she knows her city will never be the same again. Not after this. She kneels on the roof, watching debris rush past her on a river of water and mud that has consumed everything it its wake. She grasps at the glass ball on the chain around her neck, feeling it pulse and grow warm in her frigid hand. She is suddenly awake. Aware. Her ears prick and she smells the air.

A woman struggles in the water below, and the girl quickly drops to her belly and extends both of her arms.

"Hurry!" she insists, and the woman takes hold with a fierce grip. But another surge hits, and the woman lets go. A moment later she is gone.

Almost immediately, a small boy appears clutching part of a boat.

"Take my hand!" the girl screams. There is terror in the boy's eyes, and he paddles furiously toward the girl but it is no use. The force of the water is too strong.

There are more people in the water. The girl tries over and over to pull them to safety, but no one is a match for the wave. One by one, they vanish below the surface.

The girl begins to panic. Surely she can save one! Surely one of them can hang on long enough.

Someone surfaces directly below her and pleads for help, and the girl lunges for the outstretched arms and misses. A flailing hand grasps the necklace she wears and it breaks. The arm disappears, and the girl watches in horror as the glowing glass ball drops from the broken chain at her neck and then vanishes into the dark water. She throws her head back and cries out—a wild sound that is more animal than human.

Chapter One

"MORNING, KID." My aunt stands bleary-eyed at the kitchen counter. She pours herself a cup of coffee, the first of the morning. "Running a little late, aren't you?"

"It's okay," I say, pouring cereal into my bowl. "I don't have to be at the government dock until 9:00."

"Well, you don't want to dawdle." Aunt Maddie has the worst case of bed head I have ever seen. Really! On a scale of one to ten, it's about a fourteen. Instinctively, I smooth out my own hair, but it doesn't really do any good. I guess the bad hair gene runs strong in our family. Even my father's hair was ridiculous, before it all fell out, that is. Now he's just bald.

Aunt Maddie has been around for a few days, having told

Dad, who left last week for a writer's conference in Ontario, that she "needed a break from the city." But she isn't fooling anyone, especially me. I know she's just here because of my recent meltdown—the one I had when Dad brought up the subject of moving to Victoria. Again! I know things are serious with him and Anne, and I'm happy he's found someone, but there's no way I'm leaving Cowichan Bay and going to a new school next year. Dad says our houseboat needs too ·many expensive repairs, and it isn't worth hanging onto in today's market, but I disagree. Our houseboat is priceless. It's our home!

When I'm finished my cereal, my aunt snatches my bowl away and plunks it down on the counter.

"Are you trying to get rid of me or something?" I bend down to scoop up Chuck, my fat orange cat, from a patch of sun on the floor. He immediately becomes boneless, a trick he loves to perform whenever he is roused too early from one of his epic naps. I drop him on the kitchen counter, and he quickly checks out the milky puddle in my cereal bowl. His bad mood evaporates instantly. Chuck is a sucker for those toasty little O's.

"Hannah!" Aunt Maddie glares at me over her coffee cup. "What would your dad think?"

I don't answer. These days I'm not sure about *anything* my dad thinks.

Aunt Maddie looks at my backpack and frowns. "Are you sure you packed enough socks, Han?" She looks genuinely worried, as though my sock situation is a fate worse than death.

"Yes," I say. "I have eighty-seven pairs. Pure wool. Made from rare and highly prized merino sheep."

She rolls her eyes. "Come on, kid. It's a legitimate question. Tofino is a damp place, especially in March. I should know. I did field work up there for eight straight months. I grew moss between my toes and mushrooms in my boots!"

Thankfully, there's a knock on the front door—one I'd recognize anywhere. A second later the door swings open.

"Good morning, Izzy," I yell as I rinse my now-empty cereal bowl in the sink. Lots of people just walk on in our front door, it's one of the things I love most about living here. My friend, Izzy Tate, has been doing it for two years, and I never fail to recognize her distinctive knock: two loud raps. Confident and no-nonsense, just like her.

"Oh good," Izzy says, tromping into our kitchen. She's wearing gumboots with hand-painted daisies on them and an orange sweater. "You're still here. I was afraid I wouldn't get to say goodbye." Her hair has grown out since last summer, and lately, she's taken to wearing bright bandanas tied around her head. Today's is red with white polka dots. Not everyone can pull off that Rosie the Riveter look, but Isabelle Tate sure can.

"I'm glad you stopped by," I say after popping one of my aunt's toast crusts into my mouth. "I wanted to remind you again about Chuck and Poos."

Izzy sighs. "I *know*, Han. Chuck likes Cheerios, and Poos doesn't like getting his feet wet. You've only told me, like, a hundred times."

As though on cue, Poos appears outside on the deck, his mouth forming a silent "mew" to be let in. The diamond-shaped patch of white fur between his blue eyes looks a little furrowed, a sure sign he's impatient to come inside.

"Speak of the devil," Aunt Maddie says, opening the door. "Come on in, cat." She refills her coffee mug, and waves the pot in the air. "Want some java, Iz?"

"Thanks, but I have to fly." Izzy watches as Poos winds his little grey body around her ankles. "And Tyler said he'd drop me a coffee at work a bit later. I should actually go. If I don't get that kayak painted by noon, I can kiss my job goodbye!"

Tyler is Izzy's boyfriend. Ever since she met him, I don't see much of her anymore. I'm not whining really—Tyler's a nice guy—I just miss hanging out with Iz, that's all. When she's not at school, she pretty much splits her time between him and the coolest part-time job in the world: painting the boats at Blue Moon Kayaks. Right now she's doing a stylized image of Tango and Oscar, the semi-orphaned eaglets we cared for last summer. Like all of Izzy's artwork, it's going to be awesome.

A horn blasts from the marina, and Aunt Maddie jumps in the air. It's probably the coffee. Too much and she gets all twitchy.

"That's the *Tzinquaw*," my aunt says, clutching at her heart dramatically.

She would be right about that. Riley Waters, one of the original boat dwellers in the Bay, is a sea dog of many habits —one of which is to sound his boat's horn every day at 9:00 a.m. No one really knows why he does it, but no one has ever called him on it either.

"See? You are now officially late," Aunt Maddie says.

"And so am I," Izzy says, making a beeline for the door.

"I'll text you when I can!" I call after her. "Don't forget about my kitties!"

She gives me the thumbs-up and closes the door behind her. I'm not really worried; she loves the cats just as much as I do.

Two minutes later, Aunt Maddie and I are rushing up dock #5 toward the shops along the road. I feel weighed down by my loaded backpack, and the hiking boots (my aunt's old ones) that are tied to the frame slap awkwardly against my hip with every step I take.

"Slow down, Han," Aunt Maddie says when we reach the road. "I wanted to talk with you for a minute."

"But you're the one worrying about my being late," I say, not slowing down. Access to the government dock is at the other end of the village, and the clock *is* ticking.

She grabs my arm and stops me. "Come on. I just want to talk for a second."

Great. When relatives say that, it's never good. I look up and see Nell, who runs the Toad-in-the-Hole Bakery, hanging the bright yellow "Open" sign in the shop's window.

"It's about Victoria," Aunt Maddie says.

I knew it!

She squeezes my arm. "You know, Hannah, moving to Victoria isn't such a bad thing."

"I don't want to talk about it."

"Well, you're going to have to sooner or later. I spoke to your dad last night. It looks like he and Annie have found a house."

I freeze. "What?"

"It's right near Beacon Hill Park, a little cottage. Honestly, it sounds adorable. There's a fenced yard and everything. You guys could finally get a dog. I think—"

"They found a house, and I'm the last to know about it?" I feel my ears start to burn.

"He called really late last night, Han. You were fast asleep."

Nell opens the door of the bakery and gives us an enthusiastic wave. "Hey, ladies! Need a bite for the trip, Han?"

Saved by the Nell!

"Thanks, but no time," I say, walking away from my aunt. "I have to go."

"Too bad," Nell shouts. "I have a bag of warm cinnamon donuts here with your name on it."

I stop. She did, after all, say "warm" and "cinnamon" in the same sentence.

A moment later, Nell is pushing a brown paper bag into my hands. "You can never have too many donuts."

Despite my cumbersome pack, I lean in and give her a

hug. I've known Nell since forever, and the thought of living far away from the Toad is not a pleasant one at all. "Thanks, Nellie," I say. "You're awesome."

"I second that," Aunt Maddie says, half a donut stuffed in her mouth.

"Yeah, I know," Nell says. "Awesome is my middle name."

Mornings in March can be pretty chilly. At least they are in Cowichan Bay, and this one is no exception. Aunt Maddie and I bounce on our feet while we wait beside the float plane tethered at the end of the government dock.

"Where's Mike?" I ask.

"Probably up there grabbing a coffee," Aunt Maddie says, looking up toward the road. Thankfully, she doesn't bring up the subject of the Victoria move again. Instead, she begins fussing like a mother hen. She picks up the end of my scarf and winds it twice around my neck so that my chin, not to mention most of my face, pretty much disappears.

"Aunt Maddie," I plead through the wool. "I'm getting into a float plane, not a cold-storage unit!"

"Right. Sorry." She steps back and stuffs her hands into the pocket of her rain jacket. "I can't help it," she says. "You know I'm a chronic fusser. It's what I do best."

"Yeah," I say. "I know."

"Now, what about Gravol? Did you take any Gravol? You know, in case you get airsick. You've never been in a float

plane before. They can really rock around. You should probably take some. Wait. I'm sure the drugstore has—"

"I'm FINE!" I tell her. "Really. I won't get sick. I have an
ironclad stomach. Honestly."

"You're sure?"

"Positive."

"All set?" We turn to see Mike, the pilot and Aunt Maddie's
we-think boyfriend, jogging along the dock. But boyfriend
or not, it's seriously cool of him to deposit me in Tofino on
his routine flight up island. He has a travel mug in one hand
and a clipboard in the other. Aunt Maddie gives him a broad
smile and swoops in to steal the mug.

"Hey!" Mike says, scratching his full beard with his freed-
up hand. "That was mine!"

"You snooze, you lose." My aunt grins and takes a sip.
"Mmmmm. Americano, right?"

Mike pretends to be irritated, but there's a sparkle in his
eyes that totally gives him away. He gazes at my aunt like a
love-struck puppy, but after a moment he looks at me, clearly
puzzled. "Wait a second . . . aren't there supposed to be two of
you kids?"

"Two?" I say.

Aunt Maddie slaps her palm against her forehead. "Wow! I
almost forgot, Hannah. Mike's right. Mrs. Webber called last
night. She said there was a chance that—"

"Here I am," a voice says at the end of the dock.

My breath catches. What? You've got to be kidding. But it's

no joke. Walking straight toward us is my nemesis, Sabrina Webber, wearing a bright-pink pea jacket along with a sullen expression. Her blonde hair is swept back under a scarlet leather hair band, a shade identical to the oversized purse she's clutching under her arm. But it isn't Sabrina's talent for accessorizing that holds my attention, it's the coral-coloured suitcase on wheels she's pulling behind her that I can't stop staring at.

"Ah," Mike says. "There she is. Number two. You must be Katrina. All set to take to the skies?"

"Thrilled," Sabrina says in a monotone voice. "And FYI? It's *Sabrina*."

"Hey!" Aunt Maddie says, "Be nice, Sabrina."

"Figures *you'd* be on my mother's side," Sabrina says. "Why did you have to take her call last night, anyway?"

Mike raises an eyebrow at my aunt, and then frowns at Sabrina's high-heeled boots. I'm wearing my Cowichan sweater and a woollen toque, but Sabrina looks like she's dressed for one of her marathon shopping trips to the mall. And while fashionable, she doesn't exactly look ready to take on the wild beaches of Pacific Rim National Park Reserve.

"Okay," Mike says, clapping his hands together, "we've got some pretty good weather in front of us. Let's get this show on the road. You two are in for a treat. Visibility should be half-decent today. That's a rare thing on the West Coast in March."

"Joy and rapture," Sabrina mutters, booting her luggage toward him. "Can't wait."

Mike catches hold of the handle of her suitcase before it tips over. There's a crease between his eyebrows that wasn't there before, and I feel bad for him. He's pretty stoked on his float plane—a classic de Havilland DHC-2 Beaver—and the fact that he's volunteered to drop us off in Tofino on his own nickel is pretty awesome. I glare at Sabrina, but she just checks out her reflection in the window of the plane, completely oblivious. What else is new?

I can't figure it out. Why would Sabrina Webber want to give up her spring break to work with the Coast-is-Clear program on Vancouver Island's wild West Coast? Cleaning the beaches of tsunami debris from the 2011 Japanese earthquake doesn't sound like her thing at all. Sabrina is allergic to the outdoors. Nature is a dirty word to her. It just doesn't make any sense. All of a sudden, the project I've been stoked about for weeks has lost a big chunk of its appeal. I want to text my boyfriend, Max, but he's already airborne, Mexico-bound with his family for most of spring break. I don't want to ruin his stoke, and anyway, he hasn't answered my *last* text yet—the one about our probable move to Victoria.

Sabrina points at the second-hand hiking boots hanging from my backpack and wrinkles her nose. "Where'd you get *those?*"

I ignore her. If there's one thing I've learned about Sabrina, it's never to bite. She *lives* for the bite. Instead, I carry my backpack over to where Mike is loading stuff into the plane, and turn to hug Aunt Maddie goodbye. She takes hold of my shoulders and stares me square in the eye. "Now, don't stay in a snit, okay? I know cell service is sketchy up there, and I get that you're frustrated with your dad right now, but please check in as much as you can, okay?"

"I will," I tell her. "But you know Dad never checks his messages." This is absolutely true. He brags about his iPhone but he's hopeless with all forms of technology. Besides, he's still at a writers' convention in Ontario, so he probably won't even remember that I'm headed to Long Beach for spring break. His brain is like that.

"No excuses," Aunt Maddie says. "But have a great time, kiddo. The change of scene will do you good, and you're doing an awesome thing."

Sabrina smirks and leans against a dock piling. I wonder if anyone is coming down to see her off, but when I scan the marina, all I see are two men scraping barnacles off the hull of a sailboat several metres away and a couple of seagulls investigating a garbage can. They hop around a crumpled paper bag on the ground, looking for food scraps, and I'm reminded of Jack, my raven buddy. He didn't show up at breakfast today, which was weird. He rarely skips a morning visit. I wonder if he'll even notice that I'm gone? Then I give my head a shake, because as much as I adore him, he should probably get out there and make some other friends, too— some feathered ones, I mean.

"Okay, guys," Mike calls, opening the door of the float plane. "Here comes Peter. Time to board."

Peter, it turns out, is the Coast-is-Clear program facilitator, and along with Jade, a University of Victoria student, will be running the show once we get to the lodge near Tofino where we'll be staying.

"Sorry I'm a little late," Peter says with a smile. "Had to go back for this." He knocks his hand against the guitar case slung over his shoulder. "I'm not very good, but I like to bring it with me wherever I go." He's tall and lean, and his dark hair is tied in a ponytail at the nape of his neck with a leather string. I figure he must be pretty old, maybe around twenty-six.

There is a flurry of hugs and well wishes, and Mike plants a kiss on my aunt's cheek. "Text you later," he says shyly. Aunt Maddie grins from ear to ear.

Once we get inside the Beaver, there isn't much room, and both Sabrina and I sit by a window, the narrow passageway between us. I stare straight ahead, trying to figure this whole thing out, but she stiffens in her seat and says, "Just so you know, none of this was my idea, okay?"

"Okay," I say calmly. I'm used to her angry outbursts, so this one is no big surprise. She puts her ear buds in—a clear indication that she is in no mood for further conversation. Fine by me.

Ten minutes later, the float plane's engine starts up and we taxi out of the bay on big white pontoons. I stop thinking about Sabrina and start thinking about airplanes.

I peer out the window and see Riley, accompanied by Ben

North, another family friend and Cow Bay original, standing on the deck of the *Tzinquaw*, waving like mad as we taxi past. I smile. The older those two guys get, the more they seem to like hanging out together. I think they enjoy lying to each other about their glory days at sea. I wave back energetically and give them both the thumbs-up, catching a glimpse of Sadie, Ben's African grey parrot, in the cabin window. She's probably chilling out in the sink—her favourite place to be when she visits the *Tzinquaw*—and for a moment I wish I were spending my break in Cowichan Bay with all my favourite people. More than ever now, if what my aunt said about Dad and Anne finding a place in Victoria is true. If it is, then my days in Cowichan Bay are numbered.

When the float plane lifts off the water, I sneak a peek over at Sabrina. She's staring out the window at the water and swipes the back of her hand angrily across her face. But not before I see a tear slide down her cheek.

Chapter Two

I'VE NEVER BEEN INSIDE a plane like this before, and while my aunt has assured me that Mike is an experienced pilot, I still feel uneasy when the Beaver starts to pitch and tremble just fifteen minutes into our flight.

"No need to worry," Mike yells over the noise of the engine. "Just a little turbulence . . . piece of cake! We'll be out of it in a minute or two!"

"You get used to it," Peter shouts from beside Mike. "Been in planes like this my whole life! Beavers are the workhorses of the West Coast! Nothing to get nervous about!"

Easy for them to say! The plane shudders and dips, then hovers for a minute before shaking as though its wings are going to break clean off.

"Scared?" Sabrina asks me suddenly, with narrowed eyes.

"What? No!" But it's a total lie. I look out my window at the huge expanse of green directly underneath us and think about how awful it would be to crash into the Seymour Range that Mike tells us we are currently flying over. From seven thousand feet in the air, all I see is a random cluster of tiny islands, coves, peaks and bays near the coastline, and rock, trees and lakes everywhere else. If we crash, it's lights out for sure. I shut my eyes briefly, telling myself to calm down. There's no sense worrying about stuff that hasn't happened. I'm headed to Pacific Rim to clean up the shoreline. That should be what I'm thinking about, not the very remote possibility of our plane nose-diving into the side of a mountain.

I look down at the dark blue ocean, remembering the continuous news footage that played after the Japanese earthquake in Honshu—the unbelievable destruction that was unleashed when the tsunami rushed in. Dad and I watched the TV from the comfort of our living room, hardly able to comprehend the chaos we were seeing. The water just kept on coming, taking everything in its path. I can only imagine the terror that everyone must have felt, the shock and the disbelief. Some of the Japanese people watched from the rooftops of buildings, watched as their homes—their whole lives—literally got swept away. Now *those* people had reason to worry. Me? I'm in a bulletproof little plane with an experienced pilot. Clearly, I am a giant wuss.

Mike and Peter start talking to each other, but I can't hear them over the roar of the engine. Sabrina just stares at her nails, oblivious to the turbulence and noise, but her eyes are red and puffy. Our eyes meet across the aisle, and she frowns at me. "Why don't you take a picture? Seeing as you prefer looking at me over the view outside your window."

"Sorry," I say. "It's just that . . . well, are you okay?"

"Like *you* care."

And here's the funny thing, even though Sabrina is totally a piece of work, I can't help feeling a little sorry for her. I'm not completely without a heart. Last year her uncle was arrested for being part of a drug and poaching operation, and her parents have always seemed more interested in their luxury cars and trips overseas than they are in her. So despite her good jeans and good *genes*, it can't be easy being Sabrina Webber.

The engine noise evens out a little, and I shift in my seat. "Look. I know that being part of the Coast-is-Clear program doesn't seem like the kind of thing you'd want to do."

"Gee," Sabrina says sarcastically. "You think?" She picks at a fingernail. "I'd rather chew glass."

"So, how come you're here, then?"

"It's mandatory. Because I got caught."

I'm confused. "Caught?"

"You mean you haven't heard yet?" Sabrina snorts. "I thought the whole of Cowichan Bay knew."

"Knew what?" I ask.

"That I got busted for shoplifting in the village. I stole a ring from that store next to the Gang Plank."

"Earth and Sky?"

"Yeah. They're total granola freaks. Stupid thing is, I don't even like that store: all those wind chimes and Save-the-Whale T-shirts and stuff. Anyway, the owners said they wouldn't press charges if I did some kind of lame community service. And because they're eco-freaks, they wanted me to do something to 'aid the planet.' So, here I am."

"So it was go to Long Beach or go to juvenile court?" I ask.

"Something like that," Sabrina says angrily, tears threatening again. "Plus, my parents are away for spring break so they were only too happy to pack me off for the duration."

"Ouch."

"Oh, don't kid yourself," Sabrina says. "There is no 'ouch.' I gave up on 'ouch' a long time ago."

"So, why'd you do it?" I ask. The words are out of my mouth before I have time to think.

"What?"

"You know, steal the ring when you don't even like the stuff they sell?"

But Sabrina just shrugs.

Mike turns around in the pilot's seat and motions for us to lean toward him. "Hey, guys!" he shouts. "Look down there to the left! Now *that's* something you don't get to see everyday."

I peer out my window. We're not nearly as high as we were a little while ago.

"Down there," Peter shouts. "On the beach!"

I squint, and sure enough, a dark shape is ambling slowly along the rocky shoreline, followed closely by two smaller ones.

"Bears!"

"A big mama!" Peter shouts.

"Hang on," Mike yells. "I'm going circle back so Katrina can get a look."

Sabrina is clearly unimpressed with Mike, not to mention the bruins down below. "It's *Sabrina*!" she shouts back. "And there had better not be any bears where we're going!"

"Nothing to worry about." Peter yells.

"Good!"

"They mostly leave you alone, unless of course your lunch is better than theirs."

"WHAT?" Sabrina sits up straighter and glares at Peter. "You're kidding, right?"

"Nope." He laughs louder now, his eyes sparkling. "Which is why we're super OCD about garbage in the parks. Bears have good noses. They can smell a sandwich from a couple klicks away. Literally."

"Lighten up!" Mike yells over his shoulder. "Look at it out there! Look where we live! It's beautiful!"

"Everything is green," Sabrina says, but only loud enough for me to hear. "I look terrible in green."

Chapter Three

꧁ꙮ꧂

AFTER MAKING A COUPLE of wide circles over the sea, the Beaver comes to land in the harbour at Tofino. When the pontoons hit the water, the plane skids and lurches a little before Mike steers it toward the docks.

Max would totally love this. If he were here right now, he'd be talking non-stop to Mike, asking him all sorts of flight-related questions. I'm surprised by how much I miss him. I sure wish he were here, instead of being on a 737, bound for warmer skies.

The harbour is a pretty busy place. It's filled with fishing boats, a few tugs and a smattering of sailboats and pleasure crafts. We taxi up to a dock where a man is standing and waving to us. When we are about ten feet away, Mike cuts the throttle. The sudden absence of noise is strange, and my ears ring a little.

Mike jumps out the door of the plane and onto one of the pontoons. He grabs a rope and hops to the dock, placing a hand against the side of his plane. He makes it look so easy, like he's done it a thousand times (which he probably has) and jokes around with the other man while he works.

Even though the trip was only about forty-five minutes long, my legs feel a little like overcooked pasta; kind of wobbly. When Sabrina steps off the pontoon, the heel of her boot gets stuck between the planks of the dock, and she falls awkwardly on her knees beside me.

"Whoops! Okay?" Peter asks, extending a hand.

"Stupid dock!" she hisses.

More like stupid boots, you mean.

We say goodbye to Mike, who heads over to order some breakfast at a nearby cafe before continuing his trip up to Bella Bella. We walk with Peter to a nearby gas station where an old blue Chevy truck is parked. There's a sticker on the back window that says, "Haida Gwaii Rocks. Literally. (7.7 magnitude. Oct 2012)".

"She's old," Peter says, patting the door before he opens it. "1988. We're the same age, but she's a lot tougher than I am."

Sabrina climbs into the crew cab and lays claim to the whole seat with all her stuff. I sit up front next to Peter.

The secondary roads we travel on are full of potholes from the winter rains, and Peter drives pretty slowly, probably not more than thirty kilometres an hour.

"Sorry for the bumps, guys," he says. "Roads are bad this time of year, but only twenty minutes or so till we get where we're going."

The lodge we'll be staying at for the next ten days is called the Artful Elephant. It sure seems like a strange name for a place in the middle of Pacific Rim National Park Reserve. Peter tells us it's a ninety-year-old rooming house that's named after painter Emily Carr's quirky travel caravan—the one she called "Elephant." He also tells us you can get your tea leaves read from Ruth, the woman who runs the place.

We pull off onto a narrow muddy road that ends right at the stretch of beach where we will be working.

"Here we are," Peter says, cutting the engine. I stare at the Artful Elephant; a big white ramshackle house set back from the road, well settled in the overgrown grass as though it's part of the landscape. It has a glassed-in front porch, a big stone chimney running up the side of the house and an imposing set of red stairs leading to the porch. Giant ceramic pots filled with early spring snowdrops sit on most of the steps, while a multitude of tinkly wind chimes hang along the front of the house.

Peter and I climb out of the truck, and, dodging mud puddles, drag our stuff up the pathway toward the lodge. When I notice a cracked and tilting birdbath in the middle of the grass, I drop my backpack. Perched on the side of it, is a big black raven—one I'd recognize anywhere!

My smile is huge. "Buddy!" Jack hops along the edge of the concrete bowl and flaps his wings twice, his standard "hello" greeting.

I can't believe he's here! It must have taken him all day. He must have left at dawn. How did he know I was coming up here? But it's pointless to try and figure Jack out. I gave up trying a long time ago, because, well, Jack is not your average raven. I am *so* happy to see him that I almost cry.

Sabrina, still in the truck, sticks her head out the back window and gives me a dramatic eye roll. "Seriously? Your weird bird friend is here? Lame."

I ignore her, and smooth my hand over Jack's shiny blue-black feathers.

"Whoa," Peter says, coming up beside me. "This is very cool. You going to fill me in, Hannah?"

"This is Jack," I explain.

"Beautiful bird." Peter takes a step closer. "Is he a friend of yours or something?"

"Yeah. I've known him almost three years, since I was twelve."

When a big dog trots over from the house, Jack makes for a nearby cedar tree. He's not really afraid of dogs but usually adopts a better-safe-than-sorry attitude around them. This is probably because of Nell's dog, Quincy, back in Cowichan Bay. Quincy likes to full-on lick Jack whenever he gets the chance.

"Hey, Norman," Peter says, scratching the dog between the ears. Norman looks like a German shepherd, only he's jet black, with huge, oversized sticky-up ears like giant nacho chips. His nose is pinkish, and his eyes are large and sweet. He comes over to me and leans against my leg, the same way Quincy does. As luck would have it, there is a broken milk bone dog biscuit in the pocket of my jeans. Nothing new about that; I usually pack dog treats wherever I go. Norman takes it willingly and immediately sniffs around for more.

"Sorry, buddy," I tell him. "That was the last one."

He loses interest and wanders back to the house, where a woman appears on the front steps. She must be Ruth. She looks to be in her sixties, with round, red cheeks and a twist of grey hair pinned on top of her head.

"Oh good!" she says, holding up the side of her long blue skirt as she clomps down the stairs. "You're here!" She's wearing hiking boots, a heavy fisherman-knit cable sweater and a worn leather pouch at her hip.

"Hey, Ruthie," Peter says, greeting her with outstretched arms. "Good to see you!" He wraps his arms around her and gives her a bear hug.

"Well, come on in, everyone." Ruth beams, and ushers us up the stairs. "I made a big pot of corn chowder, and I just popped some cheese biscuits in the oven. They'll be ready just in time for lunch."

Cheese biscuits? My mouth begins to water. I realize I'm starving, but in the midst of all the excitement, I'd forgotten just how much. At the mention of food, Sabrina gets out of the truck, and I whisper to Jack about the seafood smorgasbord that must be waiting for him down on the beach. Flying almost 300 kilometres must have left him famished.

Ruth leads the way up the wide flight of red stairs and past a fat white cat sleeping on a couch in the sun porch. It doesn't even open an eye as we march by.

"That's Pearl," Peter says. "She's unconscious most of the time, but Ruth says she's an awfully good foot warmer at night."

I smile, and wonder whether Poos and Chuck will miss curling up by *my* feet at night. Chuck snores, and Poos licks his paws a lot, but I'm used to them.

The inside of the Artful Elephant is as funky as the outside. The walls above the dark wood wainscoting in the central hallway are covered with old-fashioned wallpaper. It's pretty faded, with raised velvety red roses all over it. The entire hallway is plastered with old framed black-and-white photographs. Some look as though they are taken here on Vancouver Island, but others show scenes of a bustling city full of traffic and tall buildings, along with huge crowds.

"The Big Apple," Ruth says as I lean in closer to inspect a photo of a street corner lit up with neon signs. "That's Times Square. I have a time-share condo in Manhattan, not too far from there, near Central Park."

"You do?" I say, and then wonder if I sound too surprised. It's just that Ruth doesn't look like the sort of person who has ever stepped away from the West Coast. She looks like part of the landscape.

"Pfffft!" Peter snorts. "That city is highly overrated."

"You've been there, too?" I ask.

"Only once. Went with Ruth two winters ago. Nothing but sirens and people and taxi cabs. I'll take the Driftwood Diner in Tofino any day. Best salmon cakes in all of B.C."

"Oh, please!" Ruth laughs. "You have no sense of adventure."

"How can you say that?" Peter grins. "I have plenty of adventurous spirit." His teeth are white and straight and when he smiles, his eyes crinkle up at the edges. "I just prefer my adventures here in B.C., that's all."

"What kind of adventures?" Sabrina looks suddenly hopeful. She hasn't taken off her fancy pink jacket yet and is standing near the old radiator where the hallway meets the kitchen.

"Oh," Peter says, "adventures in the woods mostly."

"He goes on these crazy solitary walkabouts," Ruth explains.

"What are walkabouts?" Sabrina asks.

"It's not as glamorous as it sounds," Peter says. "I just go off on my own in the woods from time to time. You know, give myself a break from conversation. Open my ears a little more. Stuff like that."

"Yeah, but what do you do for *fun*?" Sabrina asks. She stares blankly at a cobweb in the corner of the ceiling. "Hide out in the woods and eat wild mushrooms?"

"Well, in my case I guess that's pretty accurate," Peter says.

"Sounds totally boring."

"You may be right." Peter laughs.

But I disagree. I don't think Peter is boring at all.

Chapter Four

OUR BEDROOM IS AT the top of a dark mahogany staircase that has a deep burgundy carpet running up the middle. I twist the antique glass doorknob and the heavy wooden door swings open. The room is big, and the walls are painted a light yellow. There is a distinctive smell in here: that old-fashioned oil soap you use to wash hardwood floors. I stand under the sloping ceiling on one side of the room then look out the dormer window on the wall that faces the beach.

There are four twin beds, all of them wrought iron and painted bright white. They remind me of the beds you see in old movies from the 1930s, with deep, squishy mattresses and those vintage white pilly bedspreads that grandmothers seem to like so much. At least mine does.

Sabrina claims the bed under the sloping ceiling. She collapses into the middle of it with exaggerated fatigue and covers her eyes with both palms. Such drama.

I take the bed between the window and a narrow door that opens onto a little balcony with an ornate iron railing. A wicker basket full of shells and polished pieces of beach glass sits on the night table next to my bed.

I hear a clacking sound on the stairs, and a moment later Norman walks into the room. He collapses on the rug as though he owns the place. A second later he farts. Sabrina looks horror stricken.

"Hey, Norman." I walk over to give him a scratch. He's really a cool looking dog, and it's only then that I notice he has one brown eye and one blue one. Maybe there's some husky in him somewhere. He flops over on his side and yawns, hoping for a belly rub.

"Ew," Sabrina says. "How can you even touch him? I can smell him from here."

"I thought you liked dogs," I say. "What about Tiffany?"

"Tiffany is sweet and tiny and smells nice. *That* dog farts and smells heinous."

Jack, who appears on the railing of the little balcony, does not seem to share my enthusiasm for Norman either. His feathers are all ruffled up, and he fixes Norman with a beady-eyed stare through the window. Norman, however, is unfazed, and I laugh, because really, he looks anything but threatening, lying on his back with his belly exposed.

"I still love you best, Jack," I say, even though he can't hear me through the glass.

"Pathetic," Sabrina says. She stands in front of the wall mirror and smoothes out an expertly shaped eyebrow with her forefinger.

I continue to scratch Norman and smile as his eyes begin to close.

"Heard from Max lately?" Sabrina asks innocently. She applies some red gloss to her lips as she stares at me in the mirror's reflection.

"He's on his way to Mexico," I say.

"That's nice."

"I guess."

"Although I've been there, like, fifty times. It's okay, but the guys down there just won't leave me alone. You know, because of my hair. They have this thing for blondes, I guess."

"Of course," I say. "It must be so annoying." My sarcasm is lost on Sabrina, but I do start thinking about Max, and how he *still* hasn't replied to my text. I know he's on holiday and everything, but this whole moving-to-Victoria thing is pretty major for me, and I wish I could talk to him about it.

~⋇~

The dining-room table downstairs is huge; there's at least seating for twelve. The accompanying chairs are heavy wooden ones, each with a neatly stitched needlepoint cushion on its seat. My cushion is blue and green and shows a pair of otters floating on their backs in a tangle of kelp. It reminds me of the otter that's carved into the lintel over our door at home.

When we sit down to lunch, Peter tells us that the two kids from Port Alberni who were supposed to participate in the program, cancelled at the last minute. I feel deflated, and look at Sabrina, but she doesn't even appear to be listening. This is going to seriously suck. Sabrina and I working alone together for ten long, lonely days? I console myself by taking two hot cheese biscuits from the basket on the table, and smother them with butter.

Peter's girlfriend, Jade, breezes in partway through lunch, and takes the chair next to him. She's friendly looking, with straight brown hair, pink cheeks and clear, blue eyes. One of the first things I notice about her is the small tattoo of a raven on the inside of her wrist. Of course, it's a conversation starter—one that quickly leads to a discussion about Jack.

I don't tell her everything, meaning, I don't tell her the details of how I met him when I was twelve; she probably wouldn't believe me, anyway. I almost tell her about last summer, though, about how Jack helped to uncover a poaching operation in Cowichan Bay, but I catch myself in time. I mean, Sabrina is here, and her uncle is currently serving time as a result of that bust. So instead I tell Jade about how Jack helped us find some semi-orphaned eaglets, the other big event of last summer.

"What a great story," Jade says. "But I'm not surprised. Ravens are super smart, and they communicate with other animals, too. Even wolves. Some people even call them wolf birds."

"They do?" I ask. "Why?"

"Well, ravens will often warn wolves when there's a threat nearby, so it helps them hunt better. And as a thank you, the wolves will let them feast on their kills when they're done with them."

I ladle some chowder into my bowl. "And they can also mimic human speech," I say, "although Jack hasn't mastered that yet." Sabrina rolls her eyes, and I wonder if I've come off sounding like a know-it-all. I hope not. I just know a little about ravens, because of Jack.

"Did you know that this guy right here is a Raven?" Jade gives Peter's arm a squeeze.

"Excuse me?" Sabrina says in her customary monotone.

"Haida governance," Jade says. "If you are of the Haida First Nation, you belong to either the Raven clan or the Eagle clan. Peter is a Raven. Because his father is an Eagle, and his mother is a Raven."

I think about Izzy, whose mother is Cowichan, of the Coast Salish First Nation. When I first met Izzy, she wasn't interested in her mother's stories at all. Now she tells them herself. "Sounds complicated," I say to Peter.

"It is a little," he laughs. "It's a matriarchal thing. We follow our mother's lineage. Back in the day, an Eagle could marry only a Raven, and vice versa. You couldn't have two of the same."

"Oh," I nod. "Now I get it."

"God, Hannah. It's not rocket science," Sabrina says, frowning at her soup bowl.

I decide to take the high road, resisting the urge to snark back at her, but Peter comes to my defence anyway.

"No," he says, "it actually is pretty complex. It's hard to keep some families straight. Don't sweat it, Hannah." He winks at me.

⚜

We spend the rest of the day exploring the beaches we'll be working on, as well as learning a little about the native plants that grow in the area. Plants are totally Jade's passion—she's studying ethnobotany—that's the relationship between people and plants through time. Just before we head back to the lodge, she points to a black cottonwood tree growing at the edge of the forest, explaining that its sticky buds will soon appear.

"There are tons of those trees near the Cowichan River," I say. "That white seed fluff floats over the silver bridge in Duncan every April."

"That's the seeds," Jade says. "But it's the buds that smell *so* good. You can make a nice skin salve from them. People have been doing it for centuries."

"Can you believe that?" Sabrina mutters as we trudge up the beach. "No way would I *ever* put tree bud goo on *my* skin."

In the evening, Jade and Peter take us into the Big Kahuna,

a room filled with tons of books, some overstuffed couches and giant comfy armchairs that look as though they could swallow you up whole. There is a big stone fireplace at the end of the room with a hearth so wide you could easily sleep on it if you wanted to. Honestly, I've never been in a more comfortable house in all my life. The walls of this room are plastered with more photographs and big abstract paintings hanging above the fireplace, all blues and purples and teals. They remind me of the ocean.

Norman lies down in front of the fire and starts to lick his feet, and Ruth comes in with a cloth bag of knitting, to join the group. I should have known—a kindred spirit. She pulls out a skein of russet-coloured wool and starts adding stitches onto a circular needle. Must be a sweater. My fingers begin to tingle the way they always do when I'm around wool. She hands me the skein to unravel and I take the wool and get to work.

Peter dims the lights and shows us a PowerPoint presentation about Pacific Rim National Park Reserve. Then he shows us another one about the Japanese tsunami, along with actual live video footage of the day all that water rolled in. Seeing it again is no less terrifying. And now, four years later, a lot of debris has travelled across an entire ocean to our coastline. Some people say that the worst is still to come. Others say there is no way to know for sure.

When our long day draws to a close, Ruth lights a fire in the fireplace, and Peter and Jade begin a game of snooker in the corner of the room. Sabrina sits in her chair and fiddles around with her brand new iPhone. "It's dead," she says after a few frustrating moments. "Can I borrow someone's iPhone charger? I forgot to pack mine."

"Sorry, don't look at me," I say. "My phone is a hundred years old."

"There's a land line in the kitchen if you need to make a call." Jade says.

"You're kidding, right?" Sabrina flings her phone to the end of the couch. It bounces off the cushion, and lands on the rug next to Norman. "This is just great."

But I'm not listening to Sabrina. I'm listening to something outside the window, something far in the distance. Peter and Jade set down their pool cues and turn to the sound.

Norman stands up and pricks up both of his ears, and his blue and green eyes are wide and alert. Within seconds, the night air is filled with a beautiful, yet eerie sound—mournful cries that make my skin tingle as though an electric shock has run right through my whole body. It goes on for what seems like forever, and mixed in with the solemn song, is a familiar raven's cry. Right away I know that it's Jack.

"What is *that*?" Sabrina reaches for the crocheted afghan beside her and pulls it tight around her shoulders.

The air grows silent, and Jade walks over to the window to peer into the dark. "Wow," she says. "That was some beautiful song."

"Sure was," says Ruth.

Peter nods, and our eyes meet. "Ever heard wolves before?"

I shake my head. I can't even talk, but it isn't because I don't have anything to say. It's because I can't find the right words to describe what I've just heard: a beautiful sound that feels older than the forest itself.

Chapter Five

THE NEXT MORNING, the beach is practically empty. The first thing I do is look for wolf tracks in the sand, but if there were any there last night, they're long gone now.

Huge chunks of weathered driftwood sink into the sand up near the treeline, relics left over from recent winter storms. They look like big sleeping beasts whose pale, smooth bodies have been partially swallowed up by the tall dune grass. But in amongst the driftwood, is a lot of garbage. Tiny chunks of Styrofoam mostly, along with lots of plastic fragments. It all looks so out of place on this wild stretch of beach.

I push my hair under my hat and face the sea, leaning into the wind at a forty-five degree angle. It's as though the wind up here is on steroids! I hang for a couple of moments, feeling weightless before allowing myself to be blown back upright. I feel a little bit like the shrubs and western hemlock out on the point, all of them growing in the same direction, shaped by years of being hammered by the relentless winds.

It would be cool to experience a good spring storm while we're up here, and judging by the number of surfboards we saw strapped to cars in Tofino, it would seem a lot of other people are hoping for the same thing. Even so, thinking about storms gets me thinking about tsunamis and the reason I joined up with the Coast-is-Clear program in the first place. And when you factor in that the whole coast of B.C. is a seismic hot spot known as the Ring of Fire, I start feeling a little nervous. Everyone knows we're overdue for a big earthquake: a giant mega-thruster, as big as, or even bigger than the one that hit Honshu in Japan in 2011. If and when that happens, there's going to be a tsunami all right, and this part of Vancouver Island would take a direct hit for sure. What if it happens while we're here? It's totally possible. There have been lots of "burpers" in the past few months: four-or five-pointers on the Richter scale, and the 7.7 one up in Haida Gwaii a few years ago, like the sticker on Peter's truck says. Are those quakes relieving the pressure for this part of the coast or are they just a drum roll for the "big one?"

I venture down toward the water, even though we've been fully lectured on the danger of the surge channels that can occur between narrow openings in the rocky portions of the beach, and how rogue waves can appear out of nowhere to sweep you into the deep. But I have to say, I'm pretty confident around the ocean.

A heavy mist hangs over the sea, and through it I hear the familiar bark of sea lions, animals we are lucky enough to see for a couple of weeks every winter in Cowichan Bay. I spot them a few moments later, basking on a small haul-out on a rocky islet a little ways out. There must be at least one hundred of them, all barking at once like a bunch of old dogs with a bad case of croup.

I reach for my phone in my pocket to take a photo. When I look at the screen, I'm thrilled to discover a text from Max. Finally!

Hi Han. Got your msg. Sorry 2 take so long
2 answer. Sucks about Victoria stuff.
But close 2 your fave resto — Figaro's. LOL!
Hot here. Stoked 2 surf. Later. X

I read the text again, and fight back the sting I feel in my eyes. Really? Sucks about Victoria stuff? That's it? I shove my phone angrily in my pocket and mash my hat down on my head. Whatever.

I work quickly and efficiently, chucking scrap after scrap of garbage into my bags while Sabrina, Peter and Jade work the other end of the beach. I decide that I like being on my own for now, surrounded by the sound of wind and gulls and those comical croaky sea lions.

The next time I look up from filling my bag, the others are

even farther away, not much more than specks at the end of the beach. Peter waves to me and I wave back, but thankfully, they stay where they are.

My hair is covered with tiny water droplets, and I have to keep wiping away the moisture that forms on the end of my nose. I hate to admit it, but Aunt Maddie was right. It *is* wet here, and even though it isn't raining, the dampness finds its way into all of my clothes. It's going to feel great to sit on the warmed river stones of the hearth in the Big Kahuna when we stop for lunch.

There is a loud "caw" overhead, and Jack swoops down to pick something up off the beach in front of me. He flies straight up in the air only to release it, and whatever it is bounces off the rocks. It looks like a ratty piece of dried-up seaweed to me, but never a dull moment for a hungry raven, I guess. As if on cue, Ruth rings a bell from the porch of the Artful Elephant.

"Woohooo!" Peter hoots, jogging toward me on the beach with Jade not far behind. "Quittin' time!"

His long hair is wet against his neck, and his boots are caked with mud and sand. "I don't know about you," he says with twinkling eyes, "but I'm starving."

"Same here," Jade and I say in unison.

We walk up the beach to the wooden steps that lead to the deck of the Artful Elephant. When I look back over my shoulder, I see Sabrina lagging behind, dragging a mostly empty garbage bag, along with her feet. She's wearing a white-belted raincoat and a pair of knee-high, bright-white hunter boots. Even out on this wild beach, she's dressed to the nines.

Lunch turns out to be homemade pizza, loaded with about fifty delicious toppings. Why does working outside make everything taste so amazing once you come inside?

"Um. I'm allergic to shellfish," Sabrina says rudely, eyeing the shrimp on the pizza.

"Oh no!" Ruth jumps up from the table. "Don't worry, I'm sure I have some leftover soup in the fridge. It's no trouble at all to heat some up and—"

"No thanks. We had that yesterday; it was cream-based. I don't do dairy well, either." I stare at Sabrina, unsure of whether or not she's telling the truth. She could be playing one of her mind games. I wouldn't put it past her. She's pretty good at that sort of thing.

"You seemed to *do* dairy just fine the other day when you had all that whipping cream on your hot chocolate in the Salty Dog," I say, helping myself to a piece of pizza.

"It was a *soy* latte," Sabrina says defensively, "and there was definitely no whip."

Someone knocks at the front door, and Norman begins barking furiously in the hallway. I notice the hackles on his back are raised a little.

"Shush, Norman!" Ruth says, swatting him with her napkin on her way to the door. But Norman doesn't shush. If anything, he barks even louder.

There are some muffled voices, and Norman is quickly sent to another room. When Ruth returns, a girl carrying a red backpack follows close behind her.

"Everyone?" Ruth says, "This is Kimiko. She's a little late to arrive but she'll be joining in with you guys as part of the clean-up crew."

Kimiko is stunningly beautiful, and looks to be around seventeen or eighteen. She's Japanese, with porcelain skin and luminous amber-coloured eyes that twinkle even though she's not even smiling. Her shining black hair is braided: four on either side of her head, gathered into two ponytails.

"Hello," she says quietly, tugging at the hem of her purple sweater. She sets her pack down against one of the armchairs at the edge of the kitchen. "I'm really sorry to interrupt your meal." She pulls a crisp, white lace-edged handkerchief out of the pocket of her green cargo pants and dabs at the spots of rain on her face.

Handkerchiefs? Who uses handkerchiefs anymore?

"Interrupt?" Ruth snorts. "Don't be silly. We're pretty informal around here. Just roll up your sleeves and dig in."

Kimiko sits on the other side of Peter, and I notice that Sabrina looks anything but impressed with the arrival of this exotic-looking newcomer. Her cheeks are red and she begins picking shrimp off a slice of pizza.

"How long are you staying in Canada?" Ruth asks.

"Oh, I'm just visiting here for just a little while, to see the West Coast. But I heard about the Coast-is-Clear program in Tofino. I thought it seemed like a good thing to do. So I called the number and talked with Peter."

Peter nods and smiles, his mouth full of pizza.

"Well, that's awfully decent of you," Sabrina says sarcastically. "I can think of a million things I'd rather do than pick wet, mouldy Styrofoam off a beach in the rain on *my* spring break."

"I won't mind," Kimiko says thoughtfully. "Vancouver Island is so lovely, and I like the big trees."

"At my house," Sabrina snorts, "we have hired help to clean up any garbage we leave behind."

Peter ignores Sabrina and turns to Kimiko. "Well, the way I see it? We all share the planet, so if everyone pitches in, it's a win-win, right?"

Sabrina rolls her eyes and flicks a shrimp off her slice of pizza with her fork. "Oh, *pleeease*! Gag me. You're as bad as Hannah. You both sound like walking inspirational posters."

I'm speechless, but Peter just laughs it off. Kimiko, on the other hand, stares at Sabrina for a long time, a look of confusion on her face.

"After lunch, the girls will show you your room, Kimiko," Ruth says, pouring our new team member some tea. "You'll be bunking in with them."

"Oh," Kimiko says with a dazzling smile. "We will be sharing a room?" Her eyes dance and she starts in on a piece of pizza as though she hasn't eaten in a week. "How wonderful! We will be like sisters!"

Even though Kimiko must be a few years older than me, her enthusiasm is childlike, and I grin at her. Sabrina, on the other hand, just drums her fingers on the tabletop.

"Right," she says. "Sisters. Wonderful."

❦

By the time nine o'clock rolls around, everyone is ridiculously tired, having put in a full day of bending and stooping on the beach. We all spread out in the Big Kahuna, not doing much of anything, while Peter and Jade pick away at a duet on their guitars. I recognize the song right away—some old Johnny Cash tune about a train and being in prison.

I ask if I can use the land line in the kitchen to call home. Like everything else in the Artful Elephant, the phone is old school, an avocado green one that's attached to the wall. It even has a rotary dial! I have to ask how it works, which makes me feel stupid, but how would I know? This phone is probably older than my dad. I'm amazed it still functions.

Our answering machine picks up, so I leave a quick message for Aunt Maddie, and then one for Izzy, nagging her about Chuck and Poos. After I hang up, I grab my almost-dry boots from the mat by the door.

"Where are you off to?" Ruth asks, looking up from her book.

"I just want to see the beach in the dark," I tell her. "Just for a couple of minutes. That's okay, isn't it?"

"Well, stay back from the water, Hannah. The wind out there is very unpredictable this time of year."

"Okay. I'll be careful."

As soon as I'm outside, my cheeks sting from the salt spray that hangs in the air. I pull my hood up over my head and trudge down the steps to the beach. There's no moon tonight, but I can see where I'm going from the dull glow cast by the porch light.

I don't need to go very far. It's enough to sit on a piece of driftwood and just breathe deeply of the sea air. I close my eyes, letting the sound of the waves fill up my head. The ocean here is so different from the ocean in Cowichan Bay. At home, the water is mostly unchanging—flat, and busy with houseboaters, sailboats and kayakers. Most of the sounds I hear there are generated by the businesses on the shore. The smell of the ocean there is mixed with others of gasoline, baking bread, and fish and chips from the Salty Dog Café. But up here, everything is raw and wild and fresh. I get the feeling that things here haven't changed all that much from the way they've always been.

I open my eyes, and wait for them to adjust in the dark. Soon I can see the frothy white foam that appears when the waves break on the shore. It's bright, with flecks of . . . wait. There's something else down there—something in the sea-foam—a glimmer of light that appears and then disappears as the waves break and recede. At first I think I'm imagining it, but then there's another flash of light, followed by a dark shape on the sand that appears to be chasing it.

Despite Ruth's warning, I run over to investigate. Besides, the waves aren't very big and the wind isn't too scary. There's that flash again! Yes, there is definitely a bright spot in the water. Phosphorescence? I've heard about that stuff—how you can be mesmerized by schools of tiny glowing plankton that put on an underwater fireworks show at certain times of the year. Is this one of those times? But as I get closer, I know that's not what I'm seeing.

The dark shape hops near the edge of the water and squawks at me.

"Is that you, Jack?" I say, coming closer. "Whatcha got there? What *is* that?"

He cackles again and dips his head in the foam just as another wave approaches. There it is again! Something bright; something glowing; something that appears to be caught in a piece of floating Styrofoam.

I jump back to avoid the advancing water right at the same time that Jack frees the luminous object and takes off with it. He skims the surface of the sand, a sphere of bright light flickering just below his beak.

"Jack! Wait! Come back!" But he flies high up over the beach toward the wall of trees at the top of the shore. As I stumble my way through the tangle of dune grass toward the forest, I see the faint white light halfway up a cedar tree.

"Come on, Jack," I plead from the ground. "Show me what you've got there! Please?" This is not an unusual game for us. We do it all the time. Jack is always flying off with shiny objects that he believes are worthy treasures. Most of the time, they're just coins, aluminum pop can tops, or long lost earrings. This, however, is intriguing. My first guess is that it's an LED on a key chain or something.

I watch as the tiny circle of light travels to the end of a

branch and then stops moving. I wait. Nothing happens, and I start to grow impatient with Jack. He's playing hardball this time, and he knows he can't squawk back at me. He knows that if he opens his beak, whatever is in it will fall out.

It's only when another raven cries from somewhere beyond the trees that Jack instinctively calls back. That's when the sphere of light drops through the branches and lands inches from my feet.

Chapter Six

❦

IT'S A BALL. A hollow glass ball about the size of a jumbo marble, attached to a gold chain. I pick it up, marvelling at the soft golden light that spills into my hands. It vibrates gently, and heat spreads across my palms all the way to the very ends of my fingertips.

A red spiral design encircles the bottom half of the ball, and a single black Japanese character sits just above it. I pick up the chain and dangle the ball in front of me. The chain is missing its clasp but the O-rings at either end keep the ball from sliding off. Its brightness is dazzling against the black night sky.

What *is* this thing? Did it float across the entire Pacific Ocean on that piece of Styrofoam, all the way from Japan? I take a woollen mitten from my pocket, wrap the strange glowing object inside it, and tuck it away.

Instinctively, I touch the sliver of abalone that hangs on the cord around my neck. It's the necklace I've been wearing since I was twelve-years-old, and it was given to me by Yisella, the girl I met from an earlier time—the time when I first met Jack. I smile as I remember the events of that magical summer; how special the abalone necklace had been to my new friend, and how amazed I'd been when Jack had flown through time to deliver it to me after Yisella and I had said our final goodbye. That was almost three years ago.

A sudden gust of wind wakes me from my daydream, and I pull my coat tight around me. I need to get back to the lodge before someone comes out looking for me. I pat my pocket, and though I'm not sure why, my instincts tell me to keep my find on the down low, at least for now.

When I reach the lodge, there is hot chocolate in the making. As I take off my boots in the hallway, Kimiko comes in and stands before me like a statue. "Where were you just now?" she asks, and for some reason I feel as though I'm in trouble.

"Um, on the beach?"

"Why?"

I laugh a little. "Because it's there, and I felt like it?"

"Why did you feel like it?" She leans in closer, and I look at the others, but they're all crowded around the big square coffee table in the Big Kahuna, playing some nerdy fantasy board game.

"That's a very strange question," I say, standing up.

Kimiko doesn't move—she's totally invading my space bubble—but at the same time, she looks truly confused. "It is?"

"Yeah. But the answer is simple: it's a beautiful beach, and I felt like seeing it in the dark."

"You can see in the dark?" Kimiko's eyes grow wide. "So can I!"

I squeeze past her, and place my boots on the rubber mat by the door. What is *with* this girl? By now, the others have stopped playing their board game, and are looking over at us with curiosity.

"It's true," Sabrina calls out, suppressing a smile. "Hannah has night vision."

"She's right," I say. "I've been this way for a few years now."

It isn't a complete lie. Ever since that summer in Tl'ulpalus, when Yisella taught me how to "be" in the forest, I do feel pretty comfortable in the dark.

"Did you see anything interesting out there just now?" Kimiko asks quietly.

I place my hand in my jacket pocket, resting it on top of the mitten. It's very warm, almost hot. "No," I say. "Just waves, rocks and driftwood. Standard beach stuff."

Kimiko stares at me with those strange amber eyes. I try to look away, but it's hard. There's something really different about them, her pupils especially. I can't quite put my finger on it, but all the same, it's a little unsettling.

Despite everyone's good intentions, by ten o'clock we're all struggling to keep our eyes open. Jade and Peter brief us about tomorrow's plan and then check the Weather Network for storm updates and things.

I head upstairs before Sabrina and Kimiko do, my hand in my pocket. I close our bedroom door and sit down on my bed. Then I carefully roll the glass ball out of the mitten and onto my pillow. It's *so* perfect. There isn't one chip or crack on it, despite the likelihood of it having floated all the way across the ocean on that piece of Styrofoam!

I grab my phone and snap off a bunch of photos of it from different angles, then pick it up and roll it around in my hands. The light inside it has turned from yellow to a deep orange, and it feels even warmer to the touch than it did before. Warmer, and then suddenly hot! So much so that I drop it like a hot potato on the pillow, fanning my fingers in front of me in a desperate effort to cool them.

When I hear footsteps on the staircase, I scoop up the now red-hot ball in my hands and juggle it frantically before dropping it into the I LOVE NYC mug on my nightstand. It lands with an audible *hissssss* into my cold tea, and I leap off my bed and blow on my fingers.

"What's wrong with you?" Sabrina asks, coming through the door.

I think fast. "A spider. I saw a spider in my bed."

She screams and runs into the bathroom, slamming the door behind her.

While she's gone, I take a few deep, slow breaths. "It's okay," I call out, trying my best to sound calm. "It's gone now. It's safe to come out." That's when I notice the little round scorch mark in the centre of my pillow and steam rising from my previously cold mug of tea.

Chapter Seven

WHEN I WAKE UP in the middle of the night, I'm not gonna lie, the house isn't the only thing that's a little rattled. Rain beats against the window, and the wind whistles through the entire length of the Artful Elephant, making the old house heave and groan.

I turn over and my hand brushes against the rough scorch mark on my pillow. The glass ball! I squint in the darkness. I can see a lump in Sabrina's bed, but Kimiko's looks untouched.

I reach for my phone and activate the flashlight app. I was right. Kimiko is definitely *not* in her bed. A second later I see her standing at the foot of mine!

"Sorry," she says, cool as a cucumber. "Did I wake you?"

"Why are you standing there?" I back myself up against the headboard and fling my phone down beside me. Kimiko's braids are no longer tied together; all eight of them hang down in front of her to her waist. I'm instantly reminded of that horror movie that came out when I was little—the one with the creepy little girl who climbs out of a well.

"I heard something. Outside. I came to look. That's all."

"Oh."

"You'll probably think I'm crazy, but I'm a bit nervous here." She laughs. "This is nothing like my home in Japan."

"It *is* pretty windy out there tonight," I say, allowing my shoulders to relax a little.

Kimiko twists her fingers in the lace frill of her vintage cotton nightgown. It looks very white, and in the half-light I can see there is delicate embroidery across the front of it.

"Don't worry," I say as she pads back to her bed. "It's always windy up here. It's totally a Vancouver Island thing." But then start I thinking about that tidal wave again, and wonder if Kimiko was actually in the middle of it when it happened.

"Kimiko?"

"Yes?" Her voice is calm and even.

"Were you there? I mean, in Honshu? When the tsunami hit?"

"Yes."

"Did you . . . did you lose your family?"

She hesitates for a moment. "Yes."

I try to think of the right words, but in the end I just say, "I'm sorry," because I am.

"I . . . we never saw that much of each other. My mother is a great . . . she travels a lot, and my father, well, I haven't seen him since I was a baby."

I want to ask her why, but I don't know her well enough to ask such personal questions. Anyway, families split apart all the time; it's really none of my business.

"My parents didn't stay together. And my father, well, he was never really accepted by my mother's cl . . . family. They were ashamed of him. I was taken away from him when I was a tiny infant."

"You could find him now, couldn't you? I mean, if you wanted to. There are all sorts of ways you can track family members now. If you—"

"NO!" Kimiko says suddenly. "He is dead."

Sabrina snorts a little and rolls over in her bed.

"Oh! I'm so—"

"He's dead," Kimiko whispers. "And it doesn't matter, anyway. I never knew him to begin with, so how can I miss him?"

I don't know how to respond so I don't say anything.

"Hannah?"

"Yes?"

"What is *your* father like?"

"What do you mean?"

"Tell me about him, and your mother, too. And your brothers and sisters?"

My dad. My first inclination is to tell Kimiko how angry I

am at him right now. About how he's threatening to change everything about our lives that I've come to know and love. But instead I tell her how goofy and absent-minded he is, and about the kind of books he writes, and of course, about his serious caffeine addiction.

"Caffeine?" Kimiko says. "Is that a drug?"

"Oh, come on," I say. "I know you have coffee in Japan."

She turns her pillow over and lies back down. "Tell me about your mother now."

I hesitate, but not for very long. I tell Kimiko that my mother was killed in a car accident when I was ten and how much I still miss her. How sometimes I think I can hear her talking to herself in another room, and I have to go and check it out, even though I know she isn't there.

"Sometimes I smell her, too," I say, and then realizing how weird that sounds, add, "I mean, she wore this lemon essential oil every single day. And now, when I'm sad or something, I can sometimes smell the scent of lemons. I think it's her way of saying she's still there for me, you know?" I can't believe I'm telling Kimiko all this. I hardly know her.

"I like that story a lot," Kimiko says quite matter-of-factly. "Any other family?"

"My aunt Maddie," I say. "She's my dad's sister. She's pretty awesome. And there's Nell, of course, and Riley and Ben, and Izzy and Ramona, too."

"You have so many brothers and sisters!" Kimiko says excitedly.

"No, no." I laugh. "They're my friends. They all live in

Cowichan Bay, too, but they're like family to me." My eyes begin to prickle a little, because I suddenly have a random slide show in my head of my "family" in Cowichan Bay—my home that is soon to be history.

Kimiko hesitates. "But, they aren't the same blood as you. How can they be your family?"

"Hah. I guess it depends how you define the word."

"What do you mean?"

"Well, the way I see it, a family is a group of people who love you unconditionally. You know, who are there for you through thick and thin. People who have got your back, you know?"

"My back?"

"It's an expression. It means they'll stick by you. Or, take one for the team for you." I frown. This is harder than I thought it would be. "It means that they won't give up on you."

Kimiko is silent for a while, as though she is attempting to process what I've said. "And your friends? They are all like this?"

I nod, because even though Izzy gives most of her attention to Tyler these days, and Max is off surfing in Mexico, I know they care about me. "Yeah," I say. "They are."

"You are very lucky," Kimiko says, but her voice is tinged with sadness.

"Hey!" Sabrina hisses from across the room. "Can you guys *please* shut up? I'm trying to sleep. If I don't get eight hours, I'll look hideous in the morning."

I try, unsuccessfully, not to laugh. When Sabrina is once again snoring softly, Kimiko whispers, "Is that true?"

"What?"

"What Sabrina said? If she doesn't sleep eight hours, she will become hideous?"

I'm about to make a joke, but then I realize that Kimiko is being totally serious. How can anyone be so literal? "No," I say. "That's just Sabrina being dramatic. If you want to know the truth, she's hideous most of the time."

When Kimiko has finally gone back to sleep, I decide that this has been the weirdest night I've had in a long, long time.

❧

An hour later, I'm still awake. Big waves are still breaking on the shore, and the house seems to shudder a bit with each and every one of them.

To add to my worries about tsunamis, scorched pillows and creepy girls wearing nightgowns, there's the one I have about Jack. I didn't see him before I came to bed, and while it gets windy at home in Cowichan Bay, it's nothing like this!

That's when I hear something—a bark more than a howl, but there's something different about it. It sounds close! I get up to peer through the rain-splattered window at the expanse of beach in front of me. The porch light casts enough of a glow to reveal a shape down on the sand. Something with hunched shoulders, something that is staring out to sea. I watch as it waits, and then turns toward the lodge with a loose, loping gait. It's a wolf, all right—a young one, not quite full grown. I know it's a female by the way she squats to pee near some driftwood. She's kind of skinny, and I can see some of her ribs show beneath her coat. When she jumps up onto the porch to sniff at the back door, her mottled grey fur and black-tipped tail are plainly visible. I watch as she lifts her head, and I swear she stares right at our bedroom window. She is as still as a statue.

Norman, curled up on the mat in our room, suddenly raises his head.

"It's okay," I whisper to him. "Go back to sleep."

When I look back outside, the young wolf is still there, still watching our window. Can she see me, I wonder?

I ease open a little and peek my head out. "Hey, there." At the sound of my voice, her ears twitch, but she turns and lopes off toward the beach again, then once more, sits down on her haunches in front of the churning ocean. It almost looks as though she is waiting for something. I should get a picture of her! I pad over to the nightstand to get my phone, but when I come back to the window, the wolf is gone.

The rest of my sleep is broken up and punctuated with weird dreams, and by breakfast the next morning, a familiar throbbing begins directly behind my left eye. No! Just what I need: a migraine on my second day of work.

The last one I had was on New Year's Day. Max and I were hiking up Mount Tzouhalem, but we only managed to get halfway up before we had to turn around because my head got so bad. Back at home, Max put a bag of frozen peas over my forehead and pulled the curtains closed, and later, when I was feeling better, he made me ravioli and toast. I wish he were here. I miss him.

"You okay?" Peter asks over breakfast.

"I have a bit of a headache," I say quietly. I touch my forehead and wince. Even my skin is starting to hurt.

Not today. Not today. Not today.

But as everyone starts clearing the breakfast dishes off the table, I know I'm losing the battle. When Ruth wipes off the remaining crumbs from the table, the oh-so-unwelcome waves of nausea begin to wash over me.

"What's wrong with you?" Sabrina says, pushing her chair in and banging it against the edge of the table. "You look like crap."

"Migraine," I whisper.

"Everything okay here?" Ruth asks from the kitchen door.

"Hannah has a headache!" Sabrina shouts. It feels like a punch.

"Uh-oh," Ruth says. "I bet the weather is the culprit. The barometric pressure is all over the place this week. It's probably messing with your head."

"Ummmm," I say, my stomach heaving. Suddenly, I feel worse than awful.

Ruth makes shooing gestures with her broad hands. "Go. Get yourself upstairs. If anyone can sympathize with you, it's me. Migraine is my middle name."

"It's true," Peter says. "Ruthie gets 'em all the time."

Ruth nods. "The price you pay for being psychic."

I don't know anything about that, but what I *do* know is that I need to be horizontal in a dark room before I toss my cookies all over the Artful Elephant's beautiful hardwood floors.

I limp upstairs and fall onto my bed in a grateful heap. I look at the mug on my night table, and despite my throbbing head, snatch it off the table. It still has a little tea left in the bottom of it, but the glass ball inside it has vanished!

Chapter Eight

❖

I FLIP OVER MY PILLOW. The scorch mark is still there but that's all the evidence left of the mysterious glass ball. There's nothing behind the night table either. Ignoring my pounding head, I get down on all fours and check under my bed, but all I find is a dime, some dust bunnies and a postcard to Ruth from someone named Robert in Fruita, Colorado. Where *is* it? But then I remember Kimiko, standing at the foot of my bed and how weird she was after I came in from the beach last night. My face gets sweaty and my stomach heaves. I crawl back into bed and pull the comforter right over my head.

Don't think. Don't think. Don't think. Just sleep, Hannah.

When I wake up four hours later, my headache is thankfully gone. The storm, however, has returned with a vengeance, just as they said it would. I place my palms flat against the window and feel the glass shuddering behind them. Through thick condensation, I see the tall Sitka spruce trees swaying back and forth, while big waves smash down on the shore. But there is no sign of the wolf; there is no sign of anyone else either.

I reach into my backpack and pull out my oversized sweater and another pair of the work socks that Aunt Maddie snuck into my pack. I shake out the contents of the bag, but the only thing that makes a noise as it hits the floor is a dried-up tube of lip balm. No necklace. Where *is* it?

My head feels better, but my eyes are still sensitive, and when I flip on the bathroom switch, the sudden flash of light is blinding. I squint and scan the counter. Wow. Sabrina has taken over the space, that's for sure. There's a blow-dryer on the bath mat, a hair straightener on the toilet tank, and a massive gold-zippered case stuffed with cosmetics and skin creams sitting on the floor near the cast-iron radiator. I'm not going to lie; I think about turning it upside down and going through it all. Let's be honest here; the only reason she's part of this project is because of her little shoplifting incident back home. My hand hesitates above the case, but in the end I resist the urge. Besides, if Sabrina *is* the thief, she probably has the necklace with her.

I check out the rest of the bathroom. A few soggy towels are heaped on the floor, and there are long blonde strands of hair stuck on the mirror and in the sink. Being beautiful is clearly a full-time job.

Distracted, I pick up a bottle from the counter: aloe and seaweed pore minimizer. I lean in closer to the mirror and study my face. Do my pores need minimizing? How would a person even know?

I return the bottle and turn off the bathroom light. Norman is in the hallway, sleeping on the landing with his nose on his paws. He raises his head and looks at me hopefully. When he sees I am without treats, he gives me a mournful look, thumping his tail on the wooden floor planks as I carefully step over him. This is exactly why I like dogs. They just don't care about seaweed wraps or the size of your pores.

Ruth is sitting at the pine table in the kitchen, the one that no one ever eats at, sorting through some bills.

"Well you appear to be about a million times better," she says, looking up from her notepad. "Feeling okay?"

"Way!"

"Good! Weather changes can be so nasty if you're prone to migraines. I guess I was spared this time around."

"You're lucky."

"I've just boiled a kettle of water if you'd like some tea. Help yourself to any kind you'd like." Ruth puts on a pair of glasses and holds the notebook a little closer in front of her face. The page is filled with about six columns, all of them filled with numbers. Bookkeeping. Gross. "Mugs are beside the toaster," she adds.

I measure some leaves into a stainless steel tea ball that has a small frog charm attached to the chain. Then I hook it over the edge of my mug and pour in some boiling water from the kettle. Immediately, I smell mint and ginger, and after a sip or two, the last bit of fogginess in my head clears completely.

"This is *so* good," I say as I settle into the faded floral armchair in the dining room. The sky outside looks dark and grey, and I'm not unhappy to be inside. I pull a knitted afghan up over my knees.

"Don't forget to empty your tea ball when you're almost finished," Ruth calls back.

"Why?"

"Tea leaves, silly. I'll read them for you."

"Really?" I've always wanted to have my fortune told, and after what happened the summer I was twelve, well, I'm open to almost *everything*. "Can you do it right here?" I ask.

"I can read them anywhere," she says. "I've been doing them for almost forty years."

When I'm almost finished my tea, I fish out the ball and unscrew the top, dumping the soggy leaves into the little puddle of tea in the bottom of my mug. I hand it to Ruth, who swirls it around a few times before pouring most of it out over the sink. The tea leaves stick around the inside of the mug, and when she tips it upside-down, she holds it that way for almost a full minute. I notice that her eyes are closed, and her head is tilted back a bit. I seriously hope she isn't going to go into some wiggy trance or anything.

"There," she finally says, looking at the tea leaves inside my mug. "We're good to go. Come on; let's sit at the dining room table. It's more comfortable in there."

I leave the armchair a little reluctantly, but bring the afghan with me to the dining room.

"This shouldn't take very long." Ruth spins the mug several times on the tabletop. When the mug stops spinning and the handle directly faces her, she wraps her palms around either side of the mug.

A branch cracks outside and smacks against the side of the house. I jump, but Ruth remains unfazed.

"Oh!" Ruth says suddenly, peering into my mug. "This is interesting!" She pauses for a moment, and holds the mug sideways. "Goodness! There's a whole lot going on here."

"There is?" I lean forward to sneak a look. "Like what?"

"Hang on. It isn't as easy as all that. I need to study these images for a minute."

"What images? Like actual pictures of things?"

She sighs and looks at me with her warm brown eyes. "Hannah? You have to be quiet for a minute, okay?"

"Oh," I say, blushing. "Sorry."

After what seems to be *way* longer than a minute, Ruth finally sits up straight. "Okay. We're ready."

"Is it good or bad?"

"It doesn't work like that," she explains. "But I do see some images that I think may hold some significance for you in your life. Whether they are good or bad influences, remains to be seen."

"So, what sort of images are you seeing?" I ask hopefully.

"Well, there is definitely some sort of dog here." She points to a spot halfway up the side. "See? And it's inside a circle."

I look at the spot on the mug but all I see is a clump of leaves. I guess the clump *could* be a four-legged animal. But it could just as easily be a pig, or a goat. Still, I'm no psychic. What do I know? As for the circle—it's a stretch—but yeah, I see something like that.

"So," Ruth continues, "a dog is representative of a loyal friend or companion, and the circle . . . well, it could be literal, or it could be symbolic of a successfully completed task. You know, one end finally meets up with the other, to complete a journey."

I think about the wolf I saw in the middle of the night, and of course, the glass-ball necklace with the strange red spiral on it. Both of those things could be represented by seeing a dog and a circle, couldn't they? But I don't mention either of them. Aunt Maddie told me you should never offer up details when a psychic is doing a reading for you. You're just supposed to let them tell you what they see or feel. So that's what I do.

"Is there anything else?" I ask.

She hesitates. "Well . . . actually . . ."

"Actually, what?"

"There's a number here. Yes. A nine. The number nine." Ruth looks almost as perplexed as I must look, but she says it again. "Yes, definitely the number nine."

"That doesn't make any sense to me."

"I never said it would." Ruth smiles. "And it's quite rare to see numbers. They usually don't manifest. I'm not sure about this, not at all. Then again, you never know."

"You never know what?"

"You never know . . . anything."

I slouch back in my chair and fold my arms in front of me. Are all mystics this vague?

Chapter Nine

❧

THE CREW APPEARS early for lunch. Everyone is red-faced and soggy, and it is plainly obvious that Sabrina is not impressed with the wild West Coast. Oddly enough, Kimiko looks relatively dry. In fact, it's sort of hard to believe she's even been outside at all.

Peter piggybacks Jade down the hall and dumps her on her feet, pretending his back is broken from carrying the weight of her, which is hard to believe, because she's a pretty small person.

"Kind of wet out there," he says, pulling off his coat.

Sabrina stands just inside the door, looking extremely bad-tempered. Her tight designer jeans are soaked through, and her stylish boots are beginning to show signs of stress. She takes off her gloves, pulling each finger off slowly and deliberately, staring at me the whole time, as if the rain is somehow my fault.

"It's very beautiful here," Kimiko says, to no one in particular, pulling off her boots. "The trees! They're so big. Those big ones by the sand, on the point, I especially like those."

"Sitka spruce," Jade says. "A very handy tree." She looks at Sabrina's boots and frowns. "And you could totally use some spruce pitch for those boots, girl!"

"Excuse me?" Sabrina says.

"Pitch," Peter says. "First Nations all up and down the coast used to waterproof their stuff with it. Some still do. Works pretty well."

"Um," Sabrina says. "I don't think so. These boots are Italian leather?"

"Well," Peter says, chuckling, "can't imagine your feet care much."

Sabrina continues to sulk, while Kimiko stares mindlessly out the window. Norman is still behaving strangely, pacing back and forth across the hallway; he can't seem to settle.

"Ew," Sabrina says when he eventually ventures into the dining room to hide under the table. "That dog reeks."

"His name," I say, "is Norman."

"Whatever. He's still offensive."

So are you and the half bottle of Eau du Gross *you put on this morning.*

"He's also acting like a nut bar," Peter says, reaching up to hang his jacket on a hook in the hallway. "Never known him to pass up a day on the beach." I don't say anything, but it looks to me like Norman is more concerned with Kimiko's presence than playing a game of fetch on the sand.

"Are you feeling better now, Hannah?" Jade asks, placing her hand on my shoulder.

"Much. Thanks."

She notices my mug in front of me on the table. "Hey! Did Ruth do a reading for you?"

"Uh huh."

"Awesome! I hope you took notes. When she did mine, she was spot on." Jade looks over at Peter all mushy-faced, and he winks at her.

"What did she see in your cup?" I ask, even though I'm almost positive it had something to do with Cupid and love, or more specifically, Peter.

"Oh, a black bird, and a tiny heart in the corner."

"Hah," I say. "Not hard to figure *that* one out."

Peter and Jade exchange sappy, love-struck expressions before peering more intently into my cup.

"So?" Peter says. "How does your future look?"

"I'm not sure," I say. "The reading was sort of cryptic, you know?"

"It can be like that at first," Jade says matter-of-factly. "Just wait it out. It'll all come together. You'll see. Ruth is seldom wrong about this stuff."

Sabrina rolls her eyes when she thinks no one is looking. But I see her. I've been watching both her *and* Kimiko ever since she came in, trying to see if either one of them looks like they might have something to hide.

❦

The rain lets up a little after lunch.

We all trudge down to the beach, the others having changed into dry clothes and especially, dry socks. Ruth insists Sabrina wear a pair of her old rubber boots, and although she's always maintained she would never be caught dead in galoshes, she puts them on.

Once I'm out on the sand, the fresh salt air feels wonderful on my face, and the last foggy remnants of my migraine disappear altogether.

I watch with wonder as Kimiko hops along the wet driftwood as though she's part cat. She leaps from the log to log, barely even touching down before she jumps to the next one—it's as though she has springs in her feet! And man, is she fast! I watch her dart back and forth, up and over, and when she jumps effortlessly to the top of a three-foot high stump from a complete standstill, my jaw drops.

"Wait. How did you do that?" I say incredulously. "You must take gymnastics or something!"

She whirls around in surprise, but stays perfectly poised on one foot. "Oh! Hi! No. I'm just . . . I'm quite sure-footed, that's all."

"Wow. I'll say!"

A fat, grey mouse scurries over her foot and down the side of the stump. In a flash, Kimiko springs onto the sand, landing on all fours, just missing the tip of the mouse's tail. She gets up quickly, brushing sand away from her knees, clearly embarrassed.

"That was crazy!" I say. "You almost caught it! What would you have done with it if you had?"

"I . . . nothing. It just . . . you know, surprised me a little."

I nod, but it seems like a strange explanation to me. No one surprised by a mouse or a snake or something would pounce on it like that, would they? But Kimiko just smiles at me. There's that strange flickering light in her eyes again. I hold her gaze until she turns and walks away, and watch her as she stops periodically to sniff the air or lean her head over as though she's hearing something the rest of us can't.

At four o'clock, it's quitting time. We arrive back at the lodge to find Ruth is making oatmeal cookies. She hums and bangs bowls around in the kitchen, refusing any offers of help, so we all chill in the Big Kahuna.

As I breathe in the scent of cinnamon, I listen to the wind whip against the tarp on the woodpile outside. *Flap! Flap! Flap!* The ocean appears to have disappeared; everything is hidden in a grey shroud of mist, rain and fog. I get up twice to try and see through it, hoping so much to see a pair of big black wings, or hear a familiar raven's call.

"Jack will be fine, Hannah," Ruth says, reading my mind as

she comes into the room. I guess she wasn't kidding when she said she was psychic.

"But it's so windy," I say. "What if we get a *really* big storm? Jack is just a bird, you know?"

"He's more than just a bird," Peter says. "He's a raven. And if a storm blows in, he'll hunker down safe somewhere. Don't worry."

I force a smile. I want to believe him.

"Could someone please listen for the stove timer?" Ruth asks. "I have to pop upstairs for a minute."

Norman trots into the room but stops dead in his tracks when he sees Kimiko curled up in the floral armchair. Their eyes lock, and Kimiko jumps up and scuttles out of the room with her back against the wall. A moment later, I hear the quiet "click" of a door closing.

While I wait for the oven timer to go off, I rub the condensation off the back door window and take a good long look for Jack. I hope Peter is right, that Jack has the sense to find some ramshackle tool shed or something to spend the night in.

And then, above the wind, I hear a yelp—a noise that is quickly swallowed up by an ear-splitting clap of thunder. A sudden torrent of rain beats against the side of the lodge. It sounds like a million tiny hammers. I try to push the back door open a crack, but the wind is too strong and I let it slam shut again.

Another cry! Norman stands by the refrigerator, eyes fixed

on the window, his tail held out straight behind him. He lowers his head, his ears twitching at the sound of my voice, but he doesn't look at me; his eyes stay fixed on the door.

I look out the window again and that's when I see it—a tawny flash in the trees—something that leaps to a stump and then jumps off to disappear into the dark cover of the forest. A smallish dog with a massive sweeping tail! No. Tails! *Wait. Get a grip, Hannah!* I must be seeing things in this storm—fog and mist and lashing rain and too much grey, complicated by the intoxicating smell of cinnamon. Or maybe I'm experiencing a migraine hangover. Is there such a thing? But it doesn't matter. I *know* what I saw. I saw more than one tail! It didn't look like a dog, and it didn't look like the young wolf I saw last night either. It looked just like . . . a fox.

Only . . . there are no foxes on Vancouver Island.

Chapter Ten

❧

"HEY, LOOK WHO I FOUND!" Peter calls from the pantry room just off the kitchen. It's a big, airy space that Ruth uses to store things like carrots, potatoes and canned preserves.

Sabrina looks up from the couch, but she isn't interested enough to investigate. I, on the other hand, push away the plate of oatmeal cookies (almost as good as Nell's, but not quite) on the kitchen table and race to the pantry. And there, on the floor, tucked in beside a huge burlap sack of flour, is Jack. Warm, dry, and seemingly, content.

"Wait! How did he get in here?" I scan the room. There are no windows, and the back door is shut tight. I open the heavy door of the oak wardrobe at the end of the pantry, looking for some kind of secret passageway or something, but the only thing inside is a big basket of onions, made even bigger by their reflection in the full-length mirror on the back panel.

"Did you find Jack?" Ruth calls from upstairs.

"I did! But how did he get in here?" I still can't believe it.

"I told you ravens are smart." Peter chuckles, pointing to the cat flap on the outside door.

"No way," I say.

"Way."

"Jack!" I hiss sternly. "Do you even know how worried I was about you?"

"What a nag, Hannah?" Sabrina yells from the couch. "You totally sound like a parent."

I ignore her, grinning as Jack gives me his best beady-eyed stare along with his double-wing-flap greeting. He even looks a bit irritated, as though I've just interrupted what was supposed to be a long afternoon nap.

There is a sound at the front door, and a minute later Kimiko appears in the hallway, all rosy cheeked with dripping braids and mud-encrusted boots.

"Good lord!" Ruth says, coming down the stairs. "You went back outside? Whatever for? You're soaked to the bone!"

"I wanted to see the beach at night," Kimiko says cheerily. "Hannah and I were talking about it yesterday." She wrings out her soaking wet braids on the mat in the hall, and that's when I notice her ears; they are tiny, slightly pointed at the tops, and lie flat against her head. Even her ears are perfect.

"What? You shouldn't wander about in the dark up here," Jade says, placing the book she's been reading down on her lap. "For safety reasons, you really need to let someone know if you're going to go outside at night, okay?"

Kimiko nods and sits down on the bench to remove her boots.

"Let us know next time, Kimiko," Ruth says. "We don't want you coming to any harm."

Kimiko's face softens. "You don't?"

"Well, of course not! Honestly, dear. You're the oddest young woman!"

Norman barks from the other room, and Kimiko's pointed ears twitch nervously behind her hair.

⁂

I can't stop thinking about the missing glass ball. I've checked the scorch mark on my pillow a million times, just to ensure I didn't imagine it. I didn't. There is no doubt in my mind that the necklace travelled across the Pacific Ocean from Japan. And now I can't even get it back to its rightful owner. Sabrina may have slippery fingers, but I can't help thinking that it's no coincidence Kimiko showed up right after that glass ball did. And as soon as she arrived, the ball disappeared.

I'm still thinking about it the next day during our break on the beach. We're drinking hot chai tea that Jade has poured from two big thermoses, and talking about the discovery of a

Harley Davidson motorcycle that washed up on the beaches of Haida Gwaii a few years ago. I remember the story, but I'm only listening with one ear.

Kimiko isn't listening at all. She's in her own world, looking toward the forest with her head cocked to one side as though she's listening for something. Despite the fact that the sun isn't out, her skin shimmers as though illuminated by some secret light source. It's almost like she glows. I can't really explain it, except to say that I've never seen anyone with skin like hers.

She shifts a little on the log and touches her bare throat with her hand. Our eyes meet for a second, and she quickly looks away. Man, she's jumpy!

"Come on, crew," Peter says finally, brandishing his mug. "Let's get back at it. Who knows what we might find out there, maybe a glass-fishing float. Those are like gold when you find them!"

"How boring," Sabrina says, bending over to rub wet sand off the hem of her jeans. "That's the last thing I would ever want to find, but Louis Vuitton, or Abercrombie & Fitch? I'd love to see the water wash *them* up on shore!"

"Who are they?" Kimiko asks innocently. "Do they live here on the coast?"

Sabrina looks at Kimiko as though she has just grown a second head. "You're kidding, right?"

I come to her defence. "Maybe where Kimiko is from, they don't have those brand names."

"Don't be so naive, Hannah," Sabrina says, sounding tired. "They're international names. Everyone knows that."

Kimiko opens her mouth to speak, but when Norman appears on the beach and makes a beeline for her, she jumps up on a huge long in a single bound.

"Impressive," Jade says.

"Really, you don't have to worry about Norm, Kimiko," Peter says, laughing. "He doesn't have a mean bone in his body."

But Kimiko doesn't come down, and when Norman tries to jump up beside her, she hops down on the other side and scurries toward the stairs that lead up to the Artful Elephant.

"I'll be back in a minute," she calls out over her shoulder. "I need to use the bathroom."

After twenty minutes, she still hasn't returned. How long does it take a person to pee, anyway? Sabrina and I leave Jade and Peter to finish the last of the tea and discuss—judging by the looks on their faces—Kimiko's sketchy work ethic.

Sabrina, who appears to be allergic to physical labour of any kind, stomps off to fire rocks into the water. I wander the beach for a bit, and fill two more bags with mostly plastic bottle fragments and random lids. Then I tie them off and lug them up to our designated spot near the treeline. Norman, my garbage buddy, stops suddenly to sniff the air, his body taut and still. When a twig snaps in the bush, he takes off, knocking me over and sending clouds of sand flying in all directions. A moment later, there is an ear-splitting CRACK, and Norman goes berserk!

"HANNAH!" Peter yells from somewhere back on the beach. "That was a lightning strike! Get over here!"

A thick spiral of smoke appears above the trees, but instead of turning around, I run up to the bushes, push them aside and see a big scorched patch on the trunk of a tall fir, clearly the source of the smoke.

Out of the corner of my eye, something moves. Something quick and tawny! A flash of fur, and . . . *tails*! Definitely more than one . . . *again*! I am *not* imagining things!

And then, there she is—a fox—right in front of me! She freezes on the ground, the missing glass ball balanced perfectly on the end of one of her *many* white-tipped tails! I can even see part of the red spiral design on it. That's how close I am!

Oblivious to the thick smoke that curls around her body, the fox stares at me with fixed, amber-flecked eyes; eyes that are oddly familiar, but she doesn't move a muscle. I stare back, but break my gaze when I notice the red-hot, sparking tip of her largest tail. It arcs protectively over the one carrying the glass ball. This is hard to comprehend. This . . . is unbelievable.

"HANNAH!!" Peter yells again, and I jump.

The fox springs to her feet, and in a flash of russet fur, is gone. All that remains are some stray sparks that sputter and die in her smoky wake. Lightning? I think not!

With a thumping heart, and shaky legs, I jog over to where everyone else is gathered at the steps to the lodge. There is absolutely no mistaking what I saw: a fox! She was right there. She was right in front of me! I could see her black whiskers. I could see the rosy tinge inside her pointed ears, and I saw all those tails. Plural! That fox is no ordinary fox. And there's nothing ordinary about that glass ball I found, either.

"Whoa, Han?" Jade says. "You're white as a ghost."

"You okay, hon?" Ruth puts an arm around me and gives my shoulder a little squeeze. "That lightning strike was close!"

Jack perches on the deck railing, beating his wings furiously. He eyes look ready to pop out of his skull, and he is clearly agitated. He's no dummy. He must have seen everything.

"You look awful, Hannah," Sabrina says. "Maybe you just aren't the hard-core outdoor girl you thought you were." She looks at Peter for some kind of affirmation, but he's watching Kimiko, who has just stepped out from the bush. Her pants are covered in sand and muck, and she has a dark sooty smudge on her cheek. When she sees us all staring at her, she quickly composes herself and walks over to us with tiny, precise steps, one hand clutching something behind her back.

"What were you doing?" Peter asks her quizzically. "I thought you went into the lodge?"

She smiles warmly. Her topaz eyes, full of light amber specks, clearly dazzle him, along with everyone else. And that's the exact moment when my blood runs cold. Those eyes . . . and the fox's eyes . . . they're identical.

She laughs. "Oh. I'm so bad to disappear the way I do. I'm so sorry. I was on my way back but I found . . . I found this outside the front door. She unfolds her left hand and a lifeless grey mouse lies in its centre, a tiny drop of blood oozing from its neck. Kimiko looks up at Ruth, who has walked over from the woodpile at the side of the house. "Your cat is a great little mouser, isn't she?" she chirps.

"Ew! That is disgusting!" Sabrina yells, but Ruth, a huge cat lover, is clearly impressed. "Oh! Pearl is lethal to vermin. Thank you so much for keeping it out of the house, Kimiko. I hate mice!"

Kimiko laughs. "But Pearl's eyes are very close together. That's the sign of an excellent mouser."

"That's what I always say!" Ruth agrees. "No one ever believes me when I tell them that."

Wait. Is this really happening? Kimiko is totally charming the socks of Ruth, who up until now, I'd pegged for the "no flies on her" type. But Ruth is obviously impressed with Kimiko's cat-savvy chatter, and looks at her as though she's some kind of rare cat-whisperer or something.

"Well," Kimiko explains, "I found it outside the door and I didn't think you would appreciate Pearl's little offering."

"And you picked it up with your bare hands?" Sabrina says, horrified.

Everyone seems satisfied with the explanation, but I'm not. "How did you get so dirty?" I ask her out of the blue.

She hesitates, but not for long. "Oh, I was digging a little hole for the mouse. You know, so Pearl wouldn't find it again and bring it back inside."

"Could you please just get rid of that thing?" Sabrina says, sneering. "And soon?"

Kimiko looks at the mouse, shrugs, and sends it sailing into the nearby bushes.

The others wander off, but I stay frozen in my spot, watching Kimiko.

"What?" She takes a step backwards.

"Your face," I say. "You have something on your face." I point to a tiny red drop of what looks like blood at the corner of her mouth.

"Oh!" she says nervously, rubbing the spot furiously with her finger. "It's probably just strawberries. I found a little patch up there." She points up toward the trees.

"Oh," I say. "Nice."

Strawberries in March? Does she think I'm an idiot?

She squats down and pretends to retie her already-tied bootlace. I catch a whiff of her hair. It smells like smoke.

Chapter Eleven

I DON'T TELL ANYONE about the fox in the woods, or the wolf in the night, but they are all I think about. When I casually ask Peter if there have ever been foxes on Vancouver Island, he says no, but if there had been, they'd most likely be left over from fur farms that were here in the early 1900s. Okay, maybe, but what about the tails?

I want to ask more, but I'm not stupid. The last thing I need is for everyone to think I've lost my marbles. So I shut up and let them keep thinking that the smoking tree on the beach was the result of a random lightning strike, even though Jack and I know that's not what went down. Not by a long shot! I know it better than anyone. That's what makes me so nervous. I touch my abalone necklace for reassurance that I'm not losing it—for a little tangible proof that I'm not living in some half-baked, Hannah-constructed, imaginary world. But it's hard to concentrate, and twice during the evening when we're supposed to be writing in our work journals, Jade busts me for zoning out.

⌘

The next morning, Peter and Jade tell us it's going to be a "study" day—we'll be updating our environmental notebooks and cataloguing some of the things we've found in the debris.

"But we have to make a run into town first," Peter says. "You guys want to come along?" Of course I jump at the chance to go; a little diversion into civilization is just what I need.

Kimiko enthusiastically opts to stay back at the lodge and make everyone sushi. When she starts assembling the ingredients on the kitchen counter, Jade goes over to investigate. "Yum. I love sushi!"

"Sticky rice, too?" Sabrina asks hopefully.

"Of course," Kimiko says, her nose twitching. She turns to me. "Do you like sushi, Hannah?"

Yeah. I like sushi. I'd also like an answer to what's going on around here.

"Sure," I say. "Can't wait."

Kimiko looks worried. "You can't? But it will take me at least two hours!"

I blink at her, trying to decide whether or not she's being sarcastic. But no, she's totally earnest.

"It's just an expression, Kimiko," I say. Has this girl been living in a cave her whole life or something? I mean, her English is really good, so it's not like there's a language barrier thing going on.

While the truck is warming up, I snitch a tiny bit of salmon from the counter, and carry it out to Jack. He's sitting calmly on the concrete birdbath, facing the woods, so I take great pleasure in sneaking up behind him. But when I jump at him, he hardly even flinches. Instead, he zooms in for the fish, snatching it from me and shaking it dramatically before swallowing it in one gulp.

He cocks his head and stares at my hand, hoping there's more where that came from.

"Let's go, guys," Jade calls out, climbing into the front seat of the truck beside Peter.

Sabrina gets into the crew cab, smoothing a blanket out on the seat before she sits down. "Dog hairs," she says. "They're everywhere."

"Speaking of dogs," I say, "can Norman come?" Norman is watching us from the red front steps, wearing his very best sad puppy face.

"Ew," Sabrina says. "Really?"

"Fine by us," Peter says.

Norman launches himself into the crew cab between Sabrina and I. But he doesn't settle, and I have to hang on tight to his collar—he keeps trying to crawl over Sabrina every time he sees something interesting out her window.

We drive through thick stands of Sitka spruce and cedar, and then past some western hemlock, all covered with grandfather's beard lichen. Salal and giant swaths of sword ferns cover the ground, making the forest appear almost impenetrable. Wow, the woods up here are intense!

Peter and Jade tell us about some of the people who live up here, like Codfish Joe and Millicent, a couple that used to be fishers, but who now sell hats on eBay, and Stinky Tom, the seventy-two-year-old retired lawyer who lives in a tree house and makes giant insect sculptures out of recycled scrap metal. Rumour has it he also barters goods and services for the 100-proof moonshine that he makes in a still on his property somewhere. I guess every town has its quirky residents. It gets me to thinking about Riley and Ben, Cowichan Bay's most infamous oddballs. And thinking about Cowichan Bay gets me thinking about our probable move to Victoria. What if it's true? What if Dad and Anne really *did* find a house near Beacon Hill Park? I'd hardly ever get to see Riley or Ben, or hang out at the Salish Sea Studio, or tease Ben's parrot, Sadie. I sigh, deciding I need to talk to my father soon and find out what's going on.

"You girls could grab a bite at the Driftwood Diner for a bit if you wanted, while Jade and I shop. Best fudge brownies on the coast."

"You're kidding, right?" Sabrina looks at Peter as if he's

lacking in the grey matter department. "Do you even *know* how many calories are in the average brownie?"

Peter laughs. "Well, these brownies are anything but average, so they probably have twice as many."

"I'm down," I say. Chocolate is always a good idea. I open the door and Norman walks over me and jumps out of the truck with a grunt.

"Junk food will catch up with you one day, you know, Hannah." Sabrina says, stepping gingerly out of the truck and dramatically sidestepping a mud puddle. "One day you're totally going to wake up and discover that you won't be able to buy your jeans at Hollister anymore."

"I don't buy them there now."

She gives my thirty-dollar jeans the old classic "up, down" stare. "Yeah. I can see that."

When we open the door of the Driftwood Diner, we're greeted by that wonderful smell that you find only in diners: the one that's equal parts coffee and french-fry grease. Awesome.

Sabrina, in fuchsia leggings, black boots and a fake-fur bomber jacket (which she says is seventies retro, but which I think is just seventies ugly) sticks out more than anyone else in the diner. But even I have to admit she can pull it off. She could pull off a paper bag if she wanted to. It's pretty annoying.

We sit down in a corner booth and a moment later our waitress appears wearing a waist-apron and a T-shirt with the Driftwood Diner logo on it.

"Hi there," she says, digging a pen out of the apron. "What are you guys having?"

I reach for the laminated menu wedged between the sugar dispenser and the napkin holder on the table. "I think I'll have some Earl Grey tea, please?"

"Sure," the girl says. She looks over at Sabrina. "Same for you?"

"Coffee," Sabrina says, studying the menu.

"Anything to eat?"

"Well, we heard the brownies are awesome here," I say.

"You heard right."

"Okay. I'd love one, please."

"One for you, too?" the waitress asks Sabrina.

Sabrina puts the menu back. "Are you kidding? No."

The waitress flips the cover on her pad and heads into the kitchen. "Okay. Suit yourself. Back in a sec."

"And can you make sure my coffee is extra hot?" Sabrina calls after her. Several people in the diner turn around to look at us, and I want to sink through the floor. The thing is, I don't think Sabrina has a clue that she's being a cow. She's always been this way, even back when we were little kids in kindergarten.

She starts blabbering on about a notorious cat fight that's gone viral on YouTube—a snippet from some *Real Housewives* TV show. But I listen with only one ear; I'm too busy catching snippets of random conversations from other tables. It's something I learned from my dad. He's always scribbling down bits of other people's conversations in his writer's notebook. It's not really like eavesdropping. Well, maybe it is, but writers seem to be able to get away with doing things like this, in the name of the craft.

A sudden screech of tires in the street makes me jump. Out in the road, a truck brakes hard to miss hitting . . . Norman! In a flash, I'm out the door, only narrowly escaping our waitress who is balancing our order on her tray.

When I get outside, the car has pulled to the curb and Norman is standing in the middle of the road, calm as a proverbial cucumber. He wags his whole back end when he sees me, and trots over to lean against my leg.

A man climbs out of the beat-up blue Honda, shaking his head. "Jeez . . . I didn't hit him, did I? Crazy dog was just standing in the middle of the road!"

"I know," I say. "I'm sorry. He's not my dog, but I—"

"Hey, no worries. I have a psycho-mutt back home myself. I'm just glad I didn't smoke him!" He squats down beside Norman and strokes his ears. Norman licks the man's face, most of which is hidden by a big beard, and then sniffs at his T-shirt, which has some First Nations art on the front—an orca.

I grab hold of Norman's collar. "I'm really sorry he got in your way." That's when I notice a red-spiralled tattoo on the man's arm, peeking out below the sleeve of his T-shirt. There's something very familiar about it.

"Well," he says, "look after the mutt, and have a nice day."

He gets back into the Honda, drives across the road, and pulls into the diner's parking lot. I decide that Norman has had enough excitement for now, and take him back to the truck.

"You better chill out here, Norman," I say, trying to sound stern. He looks at me with his big soulful eyes, then joyfully rediscovers an old bone on the floor behind the driver's seat and starts to chow down.

When I get back to the diner, the guy with the tattoo is sitting at the counter, fiddling with his camera. Sabrina is eyeing my brownie with avid concentration, her fork hovering in the air just above the plate.

"Go ahead." I say, sitting down. "Have some."

"Well, I guess *one* bite wouldn't kill me."

"Pretty sure you're safe." I pick up a knife and split the giant brownie in two, pushing one half toward her.

Sabrina's eyes threaten to jump out of her skull. "What are you doing? I said only a bite!"

I shrug, sinking my teeth into the moist and chocolaty awesomeness while I watch Tattoo Guy at the counter. Peter was right, the brownie tastes even better than it looks, and it looks good! I try to savour each bite, but even so, it isn't long before my half is gone.

"Why do you keep staring at that guy?" Sabrina says suddenly. "Do you know him or something?"

"Oh," I say. "I was just looking at his tattoo."

Sabrina narrows her eyes and studies the guy's arm. "Kind of a boring tatt, if you ask me."

Boring or not, I'm intrigued. Tattoo Guy's sleeve has ridden up a little, and I can see the whole design on his arm now. There's a Japanese character that sits above the red spiral. *That* looks familiar, too! "I like it," I say. "Maybe I'll ask him where he got it."

"Seriously?" Sabrina rolls her eyes, and licks chocolate icing off her finger. I notice that her half is gone now, too. "Like you'd ever get a tattoo, Anderson. Don't make me laugh."

"I might one day," I say.

But she's already lost interest, and has picked up her menu again to study it with renewed interest. "Holy crap! Did you know they list the caloric content of every single item on this menu?"

"No."

"Well, they do. And that brownie had over 400 of them!"

While Sabrina is immersed in her menu, I pull out my phone and discreetly scroll through the photos I've taken since I arrived. I find a close up of the glass ball necklace and zoom in until it fills the screen. I look up at Tattoo Guy at the counter and then back to my phone. I'm pretty sure the Japanese character on his arm is the same one that's on the glass ball. I *have* to get a better look.

When I slide out of our booth, Sabrina looks up from her menu with surprise. "You're not seriously going to talk to him are you?"

But I just shrug and walk over to the counter.

"Hey again," Tattoo Guy says when I sit down on the stool

next to him. "The girl with the dog. What's up?"

I feel my face grow warm. "Hi . . . I'm Hannah."

Tattoo Guy smiles, and waits for me to go on. I suddenly feel self-conscious. I hope he doesn't think I'm some kind of freak or anything.

"Um . . ." I begin. "Don't think I'm weird or anything, but, well, it's just that I saw . . . I mean—"

"Nice to meet you, Hannah," Tattoo Guy says, coming to my rescue. "I'm Marcus." He dips his teaspoon into the pot of honey in front of him, then holds it over his mug and waits.

I try again. "It's just . . . it's about your tattoo. That one." I point to his arm.

Marcus pulls his T-shirt sleeve up a little and looks at it as though he's just noticing it for the first time. "Oh. Right. Got it about six years ago."

"Cool," I say. "It's just that I think I've seen that spiral design and the Japanese character before, on a glass ball. I was just wondering what it means."

"Really?" Marcus says, continuing to stir the spoon in his mug. "On a glass ball? No kidding!"

"Yeah, I think I saw it in a movie or something," I lie.

"That makes sense." He points to the black character above the red spiral. "This," he says, "is Japanese for kitsune."

"Kitsune?"

"Yeah. The Japanese spirit fox."

Chapter Twelve

A CHILL TRAVELS THROUGH my whole body and my heart begins thumping in my chest. I look over at Sabrina who, thankfully, is still reading the menu.

"Why did you get that tattoo?" I know questions about tattoos are personal, but I ask it anyway.

"It's kind of a cool story," Marcus says. "You wanna hear it?"

Do I want to hear it? Um . . . yeah!

"Sure!" I say.

Marcus leans back and stretches his arms in front of him, the honey spoon still in his right hand. "I travelled a lot in my early twenties, and when I finally got to Japan I bought myself a motorcycle so I could explore some of the mountains. There are some crazy ones there. Anyway, at the end of my trip, I decided to rip down Mount Rokkō through the twisties, you know, hairpin turns, knee-dragging corners, stuff like that. But I came around a corner and BAM! Had to brake really hard to miss a fox. She was just standing there, right in the middle of the road! Kind of like your dog friend out there. Needless to say, I skidded out and went down."

"Were you hurt?"

"Nah, only my ego. A few dings and scratches on the bike, but nothing serious." Marcus shifts forward on his chair and finally puts the spoon on the napkin next to his mug. "So anyway, this fox doesn't move. She just stands there, looking at me with these crazy golden eyes."

"What did you do?"

"I got up and picked up my bike, but I stared right back at her the whole time. And that's when I notice she had something in her mouth—a glass ball with a red spiral on one end. Just like the one you see here." Marcus points to his arm.

"Whoa! It sounds like the glass ball I f . . . I mean the one I saw in that movie."

"It was her star ball. Her *hoshi no tama*," Marcus says.

"What's that?"

"That's what holds all the Firefox power," Marcus explains. "Kitsunes carry it with them at all times, and if they become separated from it, they lose power. And if it shatters, a kitsune can grow weak. Sometimes they can even die."

My head swims! This is pretty "out there" stuff. "What did you do?" I ask.

"Well, just like that, the fox turns and runs off. Just disappears. I didn't think much of it, not until I started up the bike again, that is. Barely got going around the first corner—couldn't have been doing more than 20 kilometres an hour—when I had to stop again and just shake my head."

"Why?"

"Because I would have been toast; a massive rock slide had filled up most of the road. If I hadn't braked for that kitsune, I'd have kept going at a hundred klicks an hour, straight into that turn." Marcus shakes his head. "I would have ridden right into those rocks. Game over. Literally."

"That's terrifying," I say.

Marcus stares off into space for a moment, clearly reliving the entire event. "The way I see it," he finally says, "that fox had my back. I was lucky. She must have been a Zenko kitsune—a benevolent one. Probably trying to earn another tail."

"Excuse me?"

"Zenko kitsunes are good kitsunes. They have to earn their tails. When they have nine of them, they're just about as powerful as they are going to get. That's when their fur turns white."

No. Way.

Even though it's hot in here, and the windows are all fogged up from the deep fryers, I shiver. My head starts to swim a little, and I grab hold of the counter to steady myself.

"Hey," Marcus says, placing his hand on my arm. "Are you okay?"

I snap out of it. "Yeah. I . . . I'm fine. It's just kind of hot in here, that's all."

"You sure?"

"Yes," I say, laughing. "Really. I'm fine." I steer the conversation away from me, but I can't stop thinking about the tea leaf reading Ruth did for me.

There's something about the number nine . . .

"You sure know a lot about kitsunes." I look down at the paper napkin I've been shredding in my lap; the paper curls have formed a small mountain on my right knee.

Marcus suddenly clears his throat, sits up straight and places his left hand over his heart. *"I will carry myself with honour. I will protect the defenceless. I will help the helpless. I will seek the good and reject evil. I will speak only the truth. I will serve the light."* He looks at me and then grins. "That's the Zenko oath. Pretty cool, eh?"

I nod in agreement. "Very."

"I studied Japanese mythology at U of T," Marcus says, "and kitsunes are pretty cool animals. Very badass."

"So, you actually believe all that stuff?"

"I'm pretty open-minded," he says with a smile, "especially when it comes to animals. I grew up around here, and two of my best buddies are part of the Nuu-chah-nulth First Nation. They believe all animals are pretty powerful."

I think of Jack, and of Two-Step and Tango, the eagles back

home in Cowichan Bay that Izzy and I cared for last summer. I couldn't agree with Marcus and his friends more. "What about wolves?" I ask, thinking about "my" wolf—the one I spotted from my bedroom window.

"Ah," Marcus says. "Wolves are special—the Nuu-chah-nulth believe they are symbolic of family."

That starts me wondering if my wolf has a family, and if she does, where they are? I remember those ribs. She must be so hungry. Is she hunting alone?

"Some of my best friends are animals," Marcus says, "and I consider my dog, Alexander, to be part of my family."

"Your dog is named Alexander?"

"Alexander the Great, formally. Alex for short."

"I have a raven friend," I say. "I call him Jack. We've been hanging out for almost three years."

"Really?"

"Yep. He actually flew all the way up here from the Cowichan Valley, just to be with me over spring break," I say. "He's very wise."

"No surprise there," Marcus says. "We should all stop talking so much and listen more to critters, I think."

"So, is that why you got your tattoo? Because you listened to that kitsune—that fox? Because she saved your life?"

"Pretty much. She had my back, to be sure."

"So . . . Zenko kitsunes aren't dangerous?"

"Not dangerous, but if there's a kitsune around, there's almost always going to be drama."

"Really?"

"Really," he says. "Firefox power is quite something."

"Fire?" I wonder if Marcus thinks I'm an imbecile, because I keep repeating his words, but if he does, he doesn't let on.

"Kitsunes and fire go hand in hand. They can actually start them with their tails. And that *hoshi no tama* they carry around—that's the source of all their power."

I grab hold of the counter again, the image of the smoking tree and the sparking tip of the fox's tail oh-so-clear in my mind. Lightning? No way. But why would a fox—a kitsune— start a random fire in the woods? And to me, that fox actually looked more scared than anything else.

A horn honks out on the street, and through the window I see Peter waving at us from the idling Chevy.

Sabrina yells rudely from the other side of the diner. "Come *on*, Hannah! Let's GO!" She pays the bill at the cash register and then walks out the door without so much as a thank you to the hostess behind the counter.

"Oh. My ride is here," I tell Marcus, standing up. "I have to go, but it was really interesting talking to you. Thanks for the story."

"Any time. It was nice talking to you, too, Hannah," he says. "See you around town."

In a daze, and overloaded with information, I walk on shaky legs to the door. Marcus calls out after me. "Hey, Hannah!"

I freeze. "Yes?"

"Make sure you keep your eye on that dog."

I smile. "Will do."

But Norman isn't the only four-legged creature I'll be watching.

Chapter Thirteen

ON THE DRIVE BACK to the lodge, I go over my conversation with Marcus in my head. It's a relief to know I'm not hallucinating. My eyes are working just fine, thank you very much, and so, it would seem, are my instincts. Right from the start, I knew there was something different about Kimiko. That glass ball I found is her star ball. What did Marcus call it? A *hoshi no tama*. It's Kimiko's *hoshi no tama*! That's what she had between her paws next to that smoking tree—something she's been without since the Japanese tsunami of 2011. Yep, there is no doubt in my mind; our newest Coast-is-Clear member is a kitsune.

I hate that I have no one I can talk to about this. Certainly not Sabrina! And Izzy? Even if I did manage to catch her on the phone, what can she do from Cow Bay? As for Max, well, Max is doing Max things: surfing and working on his tan. I wonder if he's even thinking about me at all? His last text—the one about my moving to Victoria—was casual at best.

We work all afternoon at the big dining room table—it feels nice to concentrate on photos and charts and things, but I find myself sneaking glances at Kimiko every chance I get.

It's so obvious now . . . those ears . . . very fox like . . . and those amber eyes . . . not really human eyes at all . . .

When dinnertime comes, Kimiko proudly carries out all the sushi she made while we were in town. It's the most impressive display I've ever seen. There must be at least ten different kinds. And kitsune or not, Kimiko has made a delicious meal.

"Do you like it?" she asks me tentatively.

"Ifth dewishus," I say, my mouth mostly full. I'm sampling a delicious fish cake with a red spiral design on top. It reminds me so much of the design on the *hoshi no tama*. I think I have spirals on the brain!

"My father would be in food heaven," Jade says, helping herself to a tuna roll. "He's crazy about sushi."

At the mention of the word "father," I realize again that I really need to talk to mine. I need to call him, because maybe my aunt got it all wrong. Maybe the house thing isn't a done deal after all. The more I think about it, the more I decide that's probably what's happened. Dad would have told me if something *that* huge had gone down.

"Um," I say, "will you guys excuse me? I just remembered I'm supposed to call my dad."

"Try the land line, honey," Ruth says when I pull out my cell. "The cell service out here is so hit and miss. We're in a bit of a dead zone."

"But it's long distance," I say.

"You can work it off with extra compost duty." Ruth shoots me a wink before walking off with a stack of empty platters. I wait for her to go back into the Big Kahuna before I pick up the receiver on the wall in the kitchen.

He answers on the first ring. "David Anderson." It's how he always answers the phone. Personally, I'm a fan of the plain old, "hello?"

"Hi, Dad."

"Hey! Hannah Banana!"

Hannah Banana. My dad has been calling me this ever since I was in diapers. I'm pretty sure I'll take the embarrassing moniker with me to my grave.

"Sorry I haven't called sooner, Dad. Are you still in Toronto?"

"For a few more days. I just got back to the hotel a few minutes ago—about to eat a grilled cheese sandwich. How are you doing up there, anyway?"

"Okay," I say.

There is a slight pause. "You sure about that, Han?"

"Sure. I'm fine. Just a little tired. We've been working pretty hard up here and stuff."

"Nope," Dad says. "Not buying it. Never known you to complain about hard work."

"Pardon?"

"I know you, kid. Something's up. Spill."

I sigh. "It's just . . ."

"Yes?"

"It's just that Aunt Maddie told me that you and Anne found a house in Victoria, near Beacon Hill Park. But I know she must have got it wrong, because I *know* you would have told me if it were true. Right?"

"Hannah," Dad says, and pauses. It makes me nervous, because whenever parents begin a sentence with your name after you ask them a serious question, it's never good. "Hannah . . . of course I was going to tell you, but I thought it would be best to wait until we were both back home."

"You mean Aunt Maddie's right? It's true?"

"It was too good an opportunity to pass up, sweetheart. We had to jump on it."

"So, we're moving to Victoria? Just like that? It's a done deal?"

"Not until the summer, Hannah. Not till you're finished school."

"Wait. I can't believe this! You didn't even *ask* me!" I look over my shoulder, but except for Norman, I'm the only one in the kitchen.

"We've talked about this a lot, love," Dad says. "You know the houseboat is falling apart. It would cost the earth to fix it up."

"So? Your book is a B.C. best-seller. And you got that big advance in January."

"It may be the only book I write that does well, though. I can't count on royalties."

My ears start to burn and I squeeze my eyes shut to try to stop the images of Cowichan Bay that are cycling through my head at warp speed. "This is all about Anne, isn't it?"

"What do you mean? I thought you liked Anne."

"I *do* like Anne. She's great, but—"

"Hannah," Dad interrupts. "I like Anne, too. A lot. I didn't think I'd ever find another person I'd want to share my life with."

"It's that serious?"

"Yes," Dad says calmly. "It is."

I don't say anything. I feel numb.

"Annie needs to be in Victoria, for work. You know that. But as long as I have my laptop and an Internet connection, I can work anywhere."

"But what about Cowichan Bay? What about all our friends? It's our home, Dad."

"Cowichan Bay will always be there, Hannah. And our friends will always be our friends. Moving an hour down the road isn't going to change that. Things can't stay the same forever, honey."

Tears spring from my eyes, and my nose begins to run.

"Listen," Dad says. "You're upset. I understand that. But let's not do this on the phone. We can talk more when we both get home. Okay?"

"Okay," I blubber.

"I love you, kid. You know that, right?"

"I know," I say, but I can't say it back.

I hang up the phone and wander over to the sink to stare into the black night outside. Pearl comes into the kitchen on silent paws and begins winding herself around my ankles, but when I bend over to pick her up, she darts out into the hallway.

I decide to go up to my room and spend the entire evening listening to the foghorn sounding and feeling sorry for myself. I lie on my bed and stare at the wall, unable to remember the last time I felt this lonely.

※

A loud crash from the kitchen, followed by a frantic scream interrupts my pity party. Ruth!

I'm down the stairs in a few bounds and find her standing on the kitchen counter, her back pressed flat against the cupboards. Pearl sits on the floor next to an overturned kitchen chair, casually batting around a little grey mouse with her paw as though it were some sort of fuzzy grey ping-pong ball.

"Another mouse," Ruth says, flapping her hands. "I know it's ridiculous, but I just don't think I'll *ever* get used to them!"

"Get down from there, Ruthie. It's not safe." Peter says, coming into the kitchen. He extends his hand to Ruth.

"No way! Safer up here than down there," she says nervously.

"I don't get you!" Peter shakes his head. "You can run around Manhattan by yourself in the middle of the night, but you're freaked out by tiny, harmless rodent."

"I know. It's just that they're so, so . . . quick! And sneaky!" She grimaces as Pearl suddenly scoops up the little mouse in her paw. We watch in horror as it somersaults through the air to land across the floor against the baseboard.

"Don't worry," I tell her. "I'll deal with it." I don't know why I say this, because I have no idea how a person is supposed to "deal" with a freaked-out and possibly injured mouse, not to mention a feline in hunt-mode. But luck is with me. I manage to barricade the little guy by the back door in the pantry with a dustpan just long enough to flip open the kitty door. The little grey mouse darts through it with Pearl in close pursuit.

Godspeed, little grey mouse.

"Is it gone?" Ruth asks in a shaky voice.

"It's all good. You can climb down now." It's hard not to laugh when I see the way her white knuckles are clutching at the front of her apron. She just doesn't seem like the sort of person who would be scared of a mouse. I guess looks can be deceiving.

Peter helps her down off the counter, and, once on the floor, she sticks her feet back into her slippers. "Phew! I'm glad that's over. I'm too old to be tiptoeing around on kitchen counters!" She picks up the bucket of vegetable peelings next to the sink and holds it out to me. "Be a love, Hannah? Could you run this out to the compost bin? It's probably what attracted that little intruder inside the first place."

I laugh. "You weren't kidding about owing for the long distance call. Sure thing."

The night air is cold and still. It feels more like mid December than late March. There is no sign of Pearl, or her tiny terrified rodent friend. I hope it got away. I know it is just nature doing its thing, but hey, the mouse got this far. Seems only fair it should have a second chance.

I walk to the ramshackle outbuilding where the garbage and compost bins are kept. There's a collection of old pails piled outside the door, and a tangle of hose lying across the path to the shed. It looks like an accident waiting to happen so I do my best to haul the hoses away. Then I place the bucket of vegetable peelings on the ground and pull on the chain hanging from the bare light bulb above the door. That's when I see them, the tracks on the ground. Dog tracks? They circle around the hose, and then go back toward the lodge where they stop directly under the window. They are a little different from Norman's tracks, wider somehow, and the two middle toenails point toward each other, instead of away. We did a unit on animal tracks in Environmental Science class last year. These are wolf tracks.

I whirl around, suddenly conscious of the fact that I'm not alone. And sure enough, as I peer past Ruth's property line into the shadowy forest, I hear him before I see him—hear the soft *swish, swish, swish* of his wings as they fly through the night toward me.

"There you are, buddy," I whisper as Jack lands on my shoulder. His wing brushes the side of my face, cool and smooth against my cheek. I raise my hand and stroke his tail feathers.

"You keeping busy exploring?"

He nods his head and I take that as his answer. It makes me laugh. Good old Jack.

Something moves in the forest, and Jack makes a throaty little noise from somewhere deep in his chest. The bushes part, but my feet stay rooted to the ground as she emerges from the woods, silent as a ghost.

Canis Crassodon, the elusive Vancouver Island wolf! It's the same one as before, the almost-grown female. She stops next to a giant Sitka spruce, her silver, black-tipped tail held straight out behind her. My common sense tells me to retreat slowly and get back to the lodge, but I can't seem to make myself move so I stay where I am.

The wolf's eyes are almond shaped, and they watch me watch her. I force myself to look away for a moment because I don't want her to think I'm challenging her but even so, she doesn't move.

"Who are you?" I whisper softly. She doesn't spook when she hears my voice, but she does tilt her head ever so slightly. Then she looks past me to the lodge, and raises her head.

"What?" I whisper. "Is there something in the tree?" I look up but all I see is the light in our bedroom window.

Jack jumps from my shoulder to land between us, and the wolf lowers her head to nudge him gently with her nose.

This feels surreal, like a dream. Here I am, standing in the dark with a raven and a wild wolf. It's crazy awesome! That the wolf accepts my presence here is even more so.

The light from the shed travels along the wolf's back as she circles the spruce tree, revealing flecks of blue and gunmetal-grey fur mixed in with the silver. But she is very thin, and I wonder when, and what, she last ate.

"Hey! Everything okay out there?" Ruth calls from the kitchen. In a flash both the wolf, and Jack, are gone.

"Fine!" I call out.

I dump the peelings in the big bin, run back to the lodge and place the empty compost bucket back in the cupboard under the sink.

⁂

Just as I'm drifting off to sleep, I hear howling again, but it seems so far away, as though it's travelling across the ocean. I have to concentrate really hard to hear it. I sink lower under the covers, and when it stops, I wait for "my" wolf to answer. Only she doesn't.

I can still see her standing so silently beside the big Sitka spruce, its gray-blue needles, so similar to the colour of her fur, almost iridescent under the faint glow of the porch light.

Sitka. It's the perfect name for her.

⁂

I spend the next day working on the beach in a state of high alert, watching Kimiko—watching for signs of . . . anything. I keep my eye out for Sitka, too, but there is no trace of her. No tracks. No nothing. Last night seems like a dream, and eventually I just pull down my hat and get busy doing what I came here to do: clean up.

It's *so* grey and drizzly today that halfway through the morning I dash back to the lodge to put on my favourite piece of clothing that I own—my Cowichan sweater—lovingly made for me by Izzy's mom, Emma Tate, one of the best Cowichan knitters in the valley. The design she chose for my sweater is beautiful—a raven, of course—and as soon as I have it on, I feel better. The weight and warmth of the wool is comforting; a little slice of home.

A bit later I hear the "ping" of an incoming message on my phone. It takes me by surprise because, as Ruth said, the cell service is so unpredictable. But when I open the message, my heart skips a beat. It's a text from Max! He tells me that his family is about to leave their hotel in Mexico to go trekking in some remote area for a few days, and he'll be out of range for a while. Great.

But it doesn't matter, anyway; there's no way I can talk to Max about any of this. Because if I'm completely honest with myself, I'm still not entirely convinced he always believes some of the stuff I tell him. I guess I'm thinking about what happened to me when I was twelve, the summer I found the spindle whorl and met Jack—the whole time travel thing. To this day, he says he believes me, but . . . I just don't know.

Jack appears out of nowhere and flies over my head. I stop and hold out my arm, and when he settles on it, his talons sink into the thick wool of my sweater.

"Glad to see you, Jack." At least *he's* on my side. I never have to question where *Jack's* loyalties lie. Like a champ, he hangs out all afternoon with me while I work on the beach.

When I've filled my last bag of the day, I stare out at the dark grey sea and wonder, just when exactly did my life get so crazy? Everything feels so unsettled. Unsure. To add to the drama, I am apparently sharing a room with a kitsune, to boot. Could things get any weirder?

Later that night, while everyone shares a big plate of nachos in the Big Kahuna, I sneak outside, mostly to look for Sitka. The drizzle has finally stopped, and the sound of the ocean roars in the distance.

I walk toward the beach steps and lean against the railing, gazing up at the handful of stars that wink down at me. Maybe the sky is finally clearing. Maybe we'll see some sun tomorrow. Sun would be nice.

As I walk back to the lodge, I look up at our bedroom window, and my breath catches in my throat. I can just make out the shape of Kimiko, half-hidden behind the heavy brocade curtain and still as a ghost, watching me.

Chapter Fourteen

BREAKFAST AT THE Artful Elephant is always worth getting up for. Today, there are just-out-of-the oven breakfast muffins on a plate in the centre of the table, the sort that are full of raisins and nuts and cranberries and coconut and pretty much anything else you can think of. "Kitchen Sink Muffins"—that's what Nell calls them when she makes them at the Toad-in-the-Hole. They're different every time.

The back door in the kitchen opens, and Kimiko walks in, dressed in an oversized sweater and a bright orange beret. She pulls out a chair at the dining room table and calmly smoothes out a napkin on her lap. There is condensation in her dark braided hair, and her eyes are bright and shining.

How can anyone look so good first thing in the morning? She looks so refreshed, as though she's just returned from a weekend at a high-end spa or something.

Thing is, when I woke up at 5 a.m. this morning, Kimiko wasn't in her bed again. But I guess that's no real surprise; foxes *are* nocturnal, after all.

"You sure got up early today," I say when the others are out of the room.

"I know," Kimiko says without missing a beat. "I often get up at dawn." She takes a muffin from the basket and breaks it in two on her plate.

"Dawn?" I say. "Then you got up about two hours too early."

"Oh," Kimiko says, smiling. "I already told you I have very good eyesight."

I'll bet!

"Eat up, guys," Jade says, coming out of the kitchen. "Let's get going. It looks like we might actually get some good weather today."

She's right. There are faint fingers of diluted sunlight coming through the treetops near the beach, and actual shadows have already begun to stretch across the freshly washed sand. With any luck, we'll be able to ditch our jackets by noon and just work in our T-shirts. That is going to feel great. It's been so damp up here I wouldn't be surprised if there are mushrooms growing inside my boots. But that's the West Coast for you; it's all part of its charm. At least that's what the diehard West Coasters say.

There's a thin, cracker-like crust on the surface of the sand, created by the drying wind and satisfying to crunch across. There isn't a cloud in the sky, nor is there the usual haze that normally sticks around till noon up here, even in summer. Instead, the sky is a huge swatch of blue. I tilt my head back just as a flock of Canada geese pass over, heading inland.

It isn't long before we all fall into a rhythm—all except for Sabrina that is, who appears to be in some sort of funk. *What's new?* She tells everyone she's going to stay up near the treeline, because the saltwater spray is wrecking her clothes. I watch her for a bit, but she mostly just stares at the bushes and kicks at random pieces of driftwood. There isn't a whole lot of beach cleaning going on that I can see.

I shrug, and get to work filling my own bag. There is so much plastic everywhere—tiny little pieces—probably more dangerous than the bigger floating bits because wildlife will end up eating them. Birds mostly. Peter tells us they mistake the garbage for food, and then it's game over for them. I step up my pace, and my bag is full in no time.

A piercing scream near the top of the beach makes me drop it, spilling half the contents. I run up and over the logs just as Sabrina bursts from the trees and collides with me, full on. Her travel mug lands in the sand at our feet, and I am sprayed with a shower of hot tea.

My shoulder hurts where she careened into it, but before I

can raise my arm to rub it, there is a loud grunt. A big black bear appears up ahead in the bushes. She stands on her hind legs, waving her head back and forth, trying to catch our scent. Holy crap! Since when are black bears this huge?

Sabrina looks as though she might faint, and digs her fake gel fingernails deep into the flesh of my arm. I take a step back toward the beach, hoping she will follow, but her feet are rooted to the ground.

Peter is suddenly behind us. "Sabreeeeena?" He whispers slowly as though he's talking to a two-year-old. "We need to back away very slowly, okay? That's a mamma bear, and I can hear a cub behind her."

I think Sabrina has stopped breathing.

"Sabrina?" I whisper. "Move."

She digs her nails into me even harder.

The bear drops heavily to all fours and snorts, while her cub bawls from further back somewhere. Mama waves her head back and forth, then suddenly pivots around and takes off into the bush. One final snort, and we hear both of them crashing through foliage, headed for the deep woods.

My heart jackhammers inside my chest while a searing pain rips at my arm. The stinging pain, I realize, is coming from Sabrina's unrelenting vice grip on my arm.

"Wow!" I manage to squeak, prying her talons from my flesh. She looks at her freed hand as though it doesn't belong to her body, and then starts to cry—big heaving gulping sobs that are accompanied by a whole lot of snot. "Come on, Webber," I say. "Suck it up. It's all good now."

"Oh, man! Are you guys okay?" Jade says, rushing over to us. Her face is flushed. "There's a ton of new skunk cabbage growing up there. That's prime bear food in the spring."

Peter takes one look at Sabrina, and stifles a laugh. "Relax, Sabrina. There hasn't been a black bear attack around here for decades."

"I . . . I didn't know that," Sabrina sobs, "I . . . I don't know anything!" She swats at a tear with her hand and I notice that she's shaking. "I don't know why I'm even here. I *hate* this place!"

She looks so pathetic, and I can't help feeling sorry for her. She's probably never had a family camping trip in her whole entire life.

We all walk back down the beach together, and Sabrina's sniveling lets up a little. "Well, thanks for coming to my rescue and everything," she tells us. "At least *some* of you care." She glares down the beach at Kimiko, who hasn't budged from the little patch of shade she's been working in all day.

"Kimiko!" Jade yells. "Come work in the sunshine, girl!" But Kimiko just smiles and shakes her head, no. She's been hiding in the shadows all morning. It's like she's allergic to the sun or something.

Sabrina sticks to me like glue for the rest of the afternoon. I swear there is never more than three feet between us. She keeps looking up toward the trees, then over her shoulder, and even out to sea.

"It's okay," I tell her. "Those bears are long gone by now."

"How can you know that for sure?"

"Just relax," I tell her. "And, by the way, I'm sorry I told you to suck it up. It actually *was* pretty scary."

She frown and kicks at a broken shell with her boot.

"What?"

"It's just that I feel so out of place up here." She shakes her head, and shoves her fists into her pockets. "But like *you* would understand. Adventure is your middle name."

"No," I say. "I do. I get it." And then for some strange reason I end up telling her about my dad and Anne and their plan to move to Victoria. I tell her about the house down in Beacon Hill Park, and how I'm not going to have to go to a different school in September. It feels good to get it off my chest, even if it *is* to Sabrina Webber.

"Wow," she says when I'm done talking. "You're so lucky, Anderson. I'd love to have a fresh start somewhere new."

"Hmmph," I say. "Not me."

"Strange, I always figured you were up for anything."

I blink at her. "What's that supposed to mean?"

"You know, like you could handle anything. I never figured you for the timid type."

"Well," I say. "Guess you were wrong."

And then, as though on cue, a cloud appears out of nowhere and moves directly in front of the sun.

Chapter Fifteen

FOR THE REST OF THE DAY, I work with my head down, listening to the "mellow out" playlist on my iPod. It doesn't help. With each passing hour, I seem to get farther and farther away from "mellow." And by the end of the workday, even though I have more garbage collected than everyone else and have managed to write four pages of notes in my environmental notebook, I still feel restless.

I tie off my last garbage bag and raise my arms above my head in a long stretch, leaning first to the right, then to the left. My collarbone cracks, and I rotate my shoulders back and forth until I feel the tightness let go.

The sun returns and I lift my face, feeling the immediate

soothing warmth on my cheeks. What is it about sunshine that instantly makes you feel better? Such a wonderful, temporary Band-Aid.

Still, I wish Max were here. Stupid Max and his family vacations to remote and unreachable places! But again, if I were to tell him what I know about Kimiko, he'd think I'd lost my mind for real. Izzy, on the other hand, is great with this kind of stuff. She'd be all over this mystery. I wish *she* were here.

Jack appears with a clamshell in his beak, and lands in front of me, proud of his fishy catch. He is clearly enjoying the West Coast. Up here, it's five-star dining for hungry ravens.

"Way to go, rock star," I say.

We hang out together, me chilling on a log, and he enjoying his snack. It's often like this with Jack and me. I guess that's why our friendship is so easy. We don't have to worry about saying the wrong thing at the wrong time, or hurting each other's feelings. We don't ever have to "get through" awkward silences. We just hang out, no questions asked.

That's when it dawns on me. I don't have to keep this all to myself. I can tell Jack. My secrets are safe with him. Jack always has my back—it's been that way right from the get-go. I wait until he's finished his snack, crack my knuckles, check over my shoulder for any potential eavesdroppers, and then tell him what I know. It feels strange for the first few seconds, but when Jack hops up onto the toe of my hiking boot, I know he's listening to me. I know I have his complete attention.

I tell him about finding Kimiko by my bed in the dark, and then about the missing glass ball the next morning. I tell him about the burning tree in the woods, and the multi-tailed fox I've seen twice. He blinks at me as I fill him in on Kimiko's strange behaviour, and how I now *know* the red-spiraled glass ball he found is her *hoshi no tama*. I tell him about Marcus in the diner, and lastly, I talk to him about Sitka.

"What do you know about that little wolf, Jack?" I ask. "Are you one of those wolf birds that Jade was talking about?" Jack blinks twice.

"Man, I wish you could talk," I say. "I mean, if mynah birds and parrots can do it, you could, too." He's listening to me, and I swear he smirks a little.

I know people might think that having a one-sided, heart-to-heart discussion with a windblown raven is completely messed up, but it's not. Honest. Jack listens to every single word, just the way he always does when I talk to him. I know he's taking it in, because he blinks at me in a strangely human way at just the right moments, and when I stop to pause, he leans in a little closer to me, occasionally tapping my knee with his beak as if to say, "Go on. I'm listening. What else?" Then he waits.

After I've unloaded, I feel better. Lighter somehow. Maybe I just needed to hear myself say some of these things out loud. It helps to unscramble my head, and although I'm no closer to enlightenment, it's a great relief to get stuff off my chest. Sometimes keeping secrets can really be a burden. I should have thought of Jack sooner. He always listens.

He hops up onto my arm but I can tell he's still puzzling about something; I know he's restless by the way he keeps pulling at a loose loop of wool in my sweater.

"Thanks, buddy," I say, "for listening." He opens his beak as though he's going to call out, only he doesn't. It makes me laugh.

Ruth comes out onto the deck ringing an old ship's bell, even though we're well within yelling distance. (I think she just likes the bell.)

I walk back toward the lodge—Jack riding shotgun on my shoulder—following Peter and Jade. Sabrina brings up the rear, stumbling awkwardly over driftwood in an effort to catch up to us.

I look at our shadows stretched out in front of us in the late afternoon sun, and realize Kimiko is missing from the group. Then I spot her, still up near the trees—the same spot she's been in all day.

I hang back a little, and squat behind a stumpy piece of driftwood, watching the crew climb the stairs to the lodge: first Peter, then Jade, and then Sabrina. Kimiko watches, clearly waiting until the others have gone inside the lodge. She stands perfectly still, staring first at the sky, then at the ground, and finally, her feet. When I see her shield her eyes and look up and down the beach, I shrink back down behind my stump. I watch her tentatively place a foot outside of the shadows, then race along the beach to the stairs. She gets up them in two impressive bounds! But something isn't right. As she climbs the stairs, I can't believe what I'm seeing. Kimiko's shadow is not the shadow of a teenage girl. Kimiko's shadow has *four* very distinctive legs, and several large bushy tails!

～※～

In the evening, everyone piles into the Big Kahuna to watch a movie on the big flat screen. Jade has made her specialty popcorn—a mixture involving a lot of soya sauce and freshly grated Parmesan cheese.

"Now comes the hard part," she says, setting the bowl down and reaching into a big wicker basket beside the couch. "Picking a movie. There must be at least two hundred in here!"

But I'm not thinking about what movie to watch—I'm thinking about how I'll confront Kimiko with what I know. Will there ever be a "right" time for that conversation? And how would I even start it in the first place?

While the others rifle through the box, I continue leafing through a heavy coffee table book I've been absorbed in. It's called *Ghost Wolf*, and it's all about Vancouver Island wolves. To be honest, I'd rather just keep reading.

"You really like wolves, huh?" Jade says, making a third pile of DVDs on the floor.

I look up from the pages. "What? Oh. Yeah. This book is awesome."

Kimiko eyes the book suspiciously, and then wanders over

to peer out the window, even though it's pitch black outside.

When it's showtime, I don't want to be rude, so I close the book and climb onto the couch, wedging myself in between Sabrina and Norman. After a few minutes, Sabrina elbows me hard in the ribs.

"Ow!" I say.

"Will you please quit twitching around?" she hisses. "And also, you're totally hogging the blanket."

She's right. I've been yanking mindlessly on the crocheted afghan and picking at its woolly orange fringe while Sabrina keeps trying unsuccessfully to claim a corner of it.

"Sorry," I mutter.

"Coming to watch?" Jade asks Kimiko, still at the window. "I think we've finally narrowed it down to three movies."

Kimiko jumps. "What? Oh! Of course."

"What are you looking at out there, anyway?" Peter asks.

"Stars," Kimiko says. "Just stars."

"Well," Jade says cheerily, "come on over here and help us eat this popcorn."

I don't pay much attention to the movie—a comedy about two guys on a road trip through the desert. Halfway through, I say I'm tired and that I'm going to go upstairs to bed. Everyone tries to convince me to stay, and I know I'm being a giant buzz kill, but I just need to be alone.

I get up, pick up the *Ghost Wolf* book from the table, and fake a big yawn. Sabrina looks visibly relieved, and quickly commandeers the entire blanket for herself.

I take my mug into the kitchen, rinse it out in the sink and place it in the dish drainer.

Norman follows me in, and whimpers at the back door.

"Really," I say. "You need to pee again?" I open the door, and he takes a couple of steps outside, only to come right back in to sit by the fridge.

"Change your mind?"

He's panting a little, and there's a wild look in his eyes.

I turn on the outside light and peer through the kitchen door's window. Something is out there! I hold my breath, and open the door a crack. There they are, a pair of golden eyes, glowing and still in the dark, up near the big spruce. Watching. It's her. It's Sitka again. I pull on a pair of rubber boots and slip through the door, closing it quietly behind me.

Sitka doesn't run away. The tips of her ears twitch back and forth, and her golden, black-rimmed eyes lock onto mine. I stop, remembering some things I read earlier in *Ghost Wolf*— some stuff about body language. Both Sitka's tail and head are held high. That's good. It means she isn't feeling aggressive.

I'm not sure why, but I take a step forward and then two more before I stop just off the path. Sitka doesn't move a muscle. She's watching my every move.

There is movement over my head, and a moment later Jack settles on a branch of the big spruce. The three of us watch each other, and my senses are suddenly razor sharp. I can smell the damp earth under my feet; I can see tiny beads of moisture clinging to the silver-blue spruce needles; I can hear the chattering of a small animal—a raccoon maybe—deeper into the woods, but throughout it all, I keep quiet

There is a beautiful wild creature standing silently before me, and I want to somehow stop time.

It feels like the best gift I've ever had.

Chapter Sixteen

❦

KIMIKO WALKS INTO THE kitchen just as I'm taking off my boots. "Where were you?" She picks up the teapot beside the kitchen sink and pours herself a mug.

"I had to let Norman out," I say.

Kimiko looks around the kitchen frantically.

"Don't worry. He's not here. I think I heard him in the laundry room," I tell her.

"It isn't like I'd hurt him," Kimiko says nervously. "I mean, not on purpose."

"What do you mean by that?" I ask.

There is a snuffling sound outside, and Norman barks from somewhere down the hall.

I stare at the back door.

There is a bump on the other side of it. Kimiko hears it, too, but she quickly takes her tea and disappears into the Big Kahuna.

When I stick my head out the back door, I see the black tip of Sitka's tail disappearing into the bush. And from somewhere deeper in the forest, I hear Jack calling to her.

⁂

The heat is intense. I cover my eyes with my hands but have to move them over my mouth to keep from choking. Smoke is everywhere: my eyes, my throat, and my nose. Jack is close by. I can hear him calling out to me.

Through smoke, I see the orange flicker of flames; hear the snapping and popping of burning wood. I've got to get out of here! I've got to find Jack!

I'm suffocating, thrashing around as though I'm half-blind! I flail my arms in all directions, desperate to find some familiar landmark to grab hold of, desperate to get my bearings. My arm smacks abruptly against a hard surface.

"OW!" I open my eyes in the darkness, and a few seconds pass before I realize that I'm in bed, and my wrist is sore from banging it into the wooden nightstand.

I exhale. Okay. I get it. It was a dream—a realistic, terrifying one, but just a dream. But it was *so* convincing, I can still smell the smoke. I can still hear Jack calling. I can still hear the crackle of flames consuming wood, and—

Fire! I leap out of bed. Smoke has found its way into the

room, and a flickering light from somewhere outside throws dancing shadows against the wall.

Outside on the ground, and not far from the outbuilding where the compost is kept, a structure is burning. The wood shed! Flames have crept across one end of the neatly stacked piles of split alder and cedar and have begun advancing up the sides.

Voices rise above the fire: Peter's, Jade's, and then Ruth's. I see them running back and forth with buckets, hoses and shovels, shouting at each other.

I rush over to Sabrina's bed and fling off her duvet. "GET UP! WE HAVE TO HELP! THERE'S A FIRE!"

"Whaaa? Go away! Leave me alone, Anderson. Must. Sleep." She struggles feebly to retrieve the duvet, but I'm one step ahead of her. I grab her arm, and pull her awkwardly to her feet.

"You can sleep later. There's a fire outside!"

"Are you freaking *kidding* me?" She is suddenly awake, and searches wildly for her housecoat. "Why is there a fire in the middle of the night?"

We stuff our feet into shoes and I drag her out of the room. There is no need to wake Kimiko. Her bed is empty.

When we get outside, Peter is throwing several heavy transport blankets over the woodpile, and most of the flames are smothered. Jade is wielding the hose, while Ruth smashes a shovel on the ground in an effort to extinguish the remaining sparks.

"What happened? Is everyone okay?" I say, stamping on a stray spark. I turn on my flashlight, shining the light in Peter's face.

"We're okay," he assures us. "But man, we were lucky your raven buddy made such a racket!"

I remember my dream. "Jack! Where is he?"

Jade points to a nearby fir; I shine my flashlight at the tree. Sure enough, there he is. Agitated, but okay.

"That was close!" Jade says, brushing some ash off the sleeve of Ruth's housecoat.

"It was also suspicious," Peter says. "Fires don't spontaneously start on woodpiles without a little help—not in March on the soggy West Coast.

"What happened?" Kimiko says, emerging from the trees. Her braids are all mussed up and there is black soot the side of her face.

"Where have *you* been?" Sabrina and I say at the same time.

"What do you mean?" Kimiko says. She rubs at the smudge on her cheek and looks at me with those weird, amber eyes.

"You weren't in our room," I say.

"No," Kimiko says. "I was in the downstairs bathroom, and then . . . I heard all the noise outside, so . . . here I am."

"You didn't do a very good job of washing your face," Sabrina says quickly.

I was thinking the same thing. When Kimiko ignores the comment, I look at Peter, Jade and Ruth, but they're not listening to us; they're double-checking to make sure the fire is good and out.

When everyone has calmed down, Ruth, ever cheerful, says, "Well, that's enough excitement for one night, I think. Who's up for some hot chocolate?"

And while the hot chocolate is appreciated, I can't believe I'm the only person who isn't buying Kimiko's lame explanation for her behaviour. Doesn't anyone else see the holes in her stories? I sip my cocoa while I watch Kimiko drink hers. If you ask me, she looks nervous. She drinks too fast, and she keeps setting her mug down on the table beside her and then picking it up again.

When we trickle back to our rooms, I'm halfway up the stairs before I remember I left my flashlight outside. I spy it on a stump near the woodpile. There is a smoky smell still lingering in the air, and a few blackened logs scattered on the ground; I can still feel a little heat coming off them.

I switch on the flashlight and shine it at the fir tree. The branch is empty. Jack is gone, but when I shine the beam at the ground, I see them. Wolf tracks. Fresh ones. Somehow I know they're Sitka's. They circle around the woodpile several times in both directions before going off toward the beach.

But there are another set of tracks, too. Smaller and finer, not quite the same as the wolf tracks, but not Norman's either. They too make the same circle as the others, but instead of heading toward the beach, they go straight back to the Artful Elephant.

I shut off my light, allowing my eyes to adjust to the different, more diffused light that the hazy waxing moon casts. It spills across the ocean, painting the small waves that ripple against the shore.

I blink, and then I blink again, because Aunt Maddie has always said that a person's eyes can deceive them in the moonlight. When I blink a third time, there's no mistaking what I see: trotting along the shoreline is the dark shadow of a lanky four-legged creature—a bird hopping along at its side. Jack. I know it's Jack.

I race back to the lodge, up the stairs and tiptoe into our bedroom. Sabrina and, yes, Kimiko too, are back in bed.

I'm just settling under my duvet when I see the sliver of light under the bathroom door. Someone forgot to turn the light off. I heave myself out of bed and pad over to the switch, but when I reach the door, I freeze. On the floor, are several sooty paw prints—prints that perfectly match the smaller tracks out by the woodpile.

Chapter Seventeen

❧

I DREAM ABOUT MY DAD. In it, we're hiking up Cobble Hill and he tells me that we're not moving to Victoria after all; that he's decided we should stay in Cowichan Bay and fix up the houseboat. When a tapping on the window jolts me awake, I'm so disappointed to discover I've been dreaming. I look outside. It's still dark—*really* dark. I pick up my phone from the nightstand and squint at the screen: 2:28 a.m. Really?

Tap tap tap tap.

There it is again. It's got to be Jack. He does this at home, especially when I sleep through my alarm. How he knows is a complete mystery.

"I hear you," I mutter under my breath, opening the window. But tapping isn't the only thing I hear—somebody is crying, and that somebody is standing on the balcony outside our bedroom. I look over my shoulder and vaguely make out a lightly snoring Sabrina, but Kimiko's bed is empty. Clearly, she's the "somebody."

I pull on a sweater and slip out onto the balcony. There's a big storm brewing, and its building fast. Waves slam the shore beyond the lodge, and the dark shapes of the trees bend and strain against the wind.

"Kimiko?"

She starts and turns around, drawing her blanket tighter around her shoulders.

"Why are you out here? Are you okay?"

She sucks in the air and stifles a sob.

"What's wrong?"

"Go away, Hannah." Her voice is small and fearful. "You . . . you wouldn't understand."

The moment has arrived; it's time for *that* conversation. "I might."

I can tell she's holding her breath, trying hard to keep herself from falling apart. She isn't doing a very good job.

"It's pretty wild out there, isn't it?" It's a question that I'm not expecting her to answer. "You should come back inside."

"No. The ocean is soothing. I want to stay out here."

She's a terrible liar. I very much doubt a person could survive a massive tsunami and then think of the ocean as soothing.

"Come on, Kimiko. I've been waiting to talk to you. Just tell me what's going on."

She starts to cry for real. I touch her shoulder, and she buries her face in her hands. "You *can't* help me, Hannah. Nobody can help me. Not here. I just—"

"What? You just *what*?"

"There are things you don't know about me."

Don't be so sure!

She takes another huge gulp of night air and locks her hands around the railing. "It's so awful. I'm such a freak!"

"No, you aren't."

That's when she comes unglued. "Yes, I am! I'm a pariah! It's the same wherever I go. I hate being the way I am! I hate that I've never had any real friends. I hate that people are scared of me! I hate that I don't belong."

I count to five in my head, trying to choose the right words. "That was you in the woods tonight, wasn't it?"

Silence.

"I've seen you, Kimiko. You know I have. The fox. It's you, isn't it?"

She hesitates and looks leans looks down at the ground below us. She knows I'm on to her, and for a minute I think she's going to hurl herself over the railing. "Yes."

"You can do things with fire," I say. It's a statement, not a question.

"Sometimes," Kimiko says sullenly. "Sometimes I can."

"Like the smoke near the tree the other day. That was you. I know it was."

She nods.

"And tonight? The woodpile, too?"

Another nod.

"So it's true, then," I say. "You're a kitsune."

"Yes," Kimiko says. "It's true."

I remember the mad rush to extinguish the flames, and how scary it might have been if no one had been at the lodge to put the fire out. Suddenly, I'm angry. "Why would you do something like that? Someone could have been hurt!"

Kimiko's voice is low, but there is frustration at its edge. "Don't you think I know that?"

"Well, then, why—"

"I was trying to regain my strength! A kitsune is deeply connected to the earth's elements. Fire is especially important. Kitsunes draw strength from the flames. Only—"

She stops.

"Go on," I urge.

"Isn't it obvious? I'm terrible with Foxfire! That time you saw me by the tree near on the beach, I couldn't even make a single flame, only a lot of smoke. And then by the wood-pile . . . well, it grew out of control so fast, and I got scared."

"Okay, okay," I say, placing my hand on Kimiko's arm. "I understand. It was an accident."

Kimiko faces me in the dark. She touches the chain around her neck, and pulls the *hoshi no tama* out from inside her clothing. It pulses in her hands and floods them with the same golden light I'd seen when I first found it.

"I came here to find it. I've been without it for years now. Back then I thought I would die without it, but . . . I didn't."

"And?"

"I didn't die, but I never really felt fully alive, either. It was horrible. I had no powers. Not even bad ones. But then a clan member told me my *hoshi no tama* was here. He told me I needed to take back what was rightfully mine. So I had to come here, Hannah. Because without my *hoshi no tama*, I have no—"

"I will carry myself with honour," I suddenly hear myself say. "I will protect the defenseless. I will help the helpless. I will seek the good and reject evil. I will speak only the truth. I will serve the light." Ever since Marcus recited the oath in the Driftwood Diner, I've repeated it over and over in my head. I know it by heart.

"That's the Zenko oath," Kimiko says with wide eyes. "You just recited the Zenko oath!"

I point to the *hoshi no tama*. "I learned it from someone I met recently. He had a tattoo on his arm like your star ball. It even had the red spiral and the character for kitsune on it. I asked him a bunch of questions."

"It's a common *hoshi no tama* design," Kimiko says. "Nothing special for me. I may be a Zenko kitsune, but I am a failure. And the thing is, I don't even care anymore. I might as well be dead."

"What are you talking about?" I say. "That's a terrible thing to say."

"You are naive, Hannah," Kimiko says. "It's *so* much more complicated than you know." She pauses. "Do you remember our first conversation? The one when I asked about your family? When I asked about your mother and father?"

"Of course."

"Well, my father. He has been dead a long time."

"But you don't know that for sure. I mean, for all you know, he could be—"

"He has been dead for almost 850 years."

Wait. What?

"He was mortal, Hannah," Kimiko says. "He was human. But my mother, my mother is an ancient and very powerful kitsune."

"Wait. Are you telling me you're—"

"I am not pure kitsune, but I'm not entirely human, either. I don't fit into either world. That's why my magic is so unreliable—why I make so many mistakes. I'm like a misshapen puzzle piece, the one that will never fit in well enough to complete the picture."

"But all those tails? I've seen them! You have to earn them, don't you? You couldn't have earned all those tails if you are as bad a kitsune as you say you are."

"Fluke," Kimiko says. "Fluke, and a lot of help from our clan. My mother is ashamed of me, and has always been concerned about my dishonouring her name. If I fail before all the others, she would lose respect from the clan. No, I cannot take credit for my tails. If it had just been left solely to me, I would still only have one.

I'm silent, because it feels like anything I might say will come out sounding trite.

"I have never done anything of which I can be proud," Kimiko says quietly. "Not one thing. That is why I've been trying to draw strength from fire. But I'm useless, as you can see."

"What if I helped you with the fire stuff?"

"No! I've had help my whole life. I will *never* grow strong unless I am able to do things for myself!"

"You're half-kitsune," I say, "and half-human. It's just . . . this is so hard to take in."

"Well, believe it," Kimiko says. "And know that I didn't have a choice in any of it. I would give *anything* to have a regular life like yours."

"Listen. Kimiko, if your father died over 850 years ago," I begin, "just how old does that make you?"

"Old." Kimiko sighs. "In human years, I've lived almost nine hundred years."

"No way!"

"It's true. My birthday is in a few days."

I process this information. Nine hundred years old? How would anyone even remember when they were born if they were that old? How would they remember *anything* from their past? I have a hard enough time trying to remember stuff I did when I was eight or nine.

"But you look so young. You look like a teenager."

"When I transform, I can be any age I choose," Kimiko explains. She's finally stopped crying, but her voice is still small and I have to strain to hear her over the wind. "It's the one part of the magic that I can manage. I have chosen to be this age for such a long time. It is the age I would like to be, if I were human."

"Well," I say, "what if you worked at making your magic, I don't know . . . better?"

"I've tried that. I even had an ancient teacher for a while, but even he could not help me. It's so unfair. I don't want much. I don't wish for great power. I just want to be able to trust myself and lead a normal life, like your life. I want to have friends and go shopping and to the movies. Maybe even learn to ride a horse . . ." She trails off, the tears getting the better of her once again. "I don't know why, but I've always wanted to ride a horse."

I realize just how much I take for granted. How awful it would be if I were limited the way that Kimiko is. This past Christmas, I got to spend time at 100 Mile House, with Max and his family. We stayed at his uncle's ranch, and I rode an appaloosa gelding named Buckshot every one of the five days I was there.

"A kitsune can never truly have a trusted friend. And it's even worse for a half-kitsune like me, because I am nothing more than a burden for everyone to bear—half-human, half alive."

"So don't go back," I tell her. "You're not a burden here. Just stay! I bet you could work for Ruth for a while. Or in Tofino?"

"Don't you see? That would *never* work. I have so little control over my shape-shifting. I never know when it's going to happen. And then . . . there's the Okami."

"The O what?"

"The Okami. That is our Japanese word for wolf."

"Wolves?" My pulse begins to speed up. "There are wolves in Japan?"

"There were a long time ago. They lived in Honshu, my home. The Okami spirit has always watched over kitsunes, and she is here. I've seen her several times with my own eyes; twice when I was in fox form. She is so beautiful."

"But," I say. "What does that mean?"

"The Okami always shows up with some sort of message. She must have one for me, but, because I am so useless, I am unable to understand what it is.

Sitka. Is that why she's been hanging around, because she has a message for Kimiko?

"I've seen her, too," I say. "I've been calling her Sitka."

Kimiko nods. "I will shame her if I can't understand her message." She draws the blanket higher up around her shoulders and then shakes her head, clearly frustrated. "I shouldn't have said anything about any of this to you."

"But I already knew!" I say. "I knew everything!"

"And now you know even more," Kimiko says, "and I have broken one of the most important rules among kitsunes everywhere. You see? You see how inept I am? I am nothing but a huge mistake!"

Kimiko slams her hand down on the slick metal railing of the balcony. "And your bird friend, Jack. He has seen too much, too. Oh, I have been *so* very foolish. It is so wrong that I have told you so much."

"You don't have to worry," I say. "Jack understands magic.

He's not your average raven. Trust me on that. He can help you. You just have to let him."

"*Pffffft*. Ravens are tricksters, too. And magic isn't always a good thing, Hannah," Kimiko says. "Things can get very complicated very quickly."

I kind of resent this, her assumption that magic is too complex a subject for me to comprehend. Well, maybe I don't understand kitsune magic, but I do know what I'm talking about when it comes to Jack. I decide to switch tacks. I reach up to touch the shining piece of abalone around my neck. "Do you see this?" I say, holding up the piece of iridescent shell between us. "This was given to me a few years ago by a very special friend. Jack delivered this to me from her, and believe me, it was *all* about magic then, Kimiko. I'm talking big-time magic! I couldn't tell anyone about it afterwards, because no one would have believed me, so I *know* how you feel. I know how lonely it is to be alone with a secret, but whether you like it or not, you're my friend, Kimiko, and friends help each other. That's just how the way it works."

"You're wrong," Kimiko says in a flat monotone voice. "I can't be a friend with a human being, and there's nothing left to talk about."

"So . . . that's it? You're not even going to try? What's here for you then? Are you going to hide for the rest of your life? Are you just going to randomly shape-shift and run around in the woods starting random fires?"

Kimiko looks as though I've slapped her. "I told you! That was an *accident*! I only meant to start a small flame in the shavings." She slumps against the rail. "I needed a flame! I needed strength. But then I saw the Okami watching me from the spruce tree, and I wanted to wait for her message. I didn't know the whole woodpile would go up in flames."

"Okay, okay," I say. "I shouldn't have said that. It's just that I—"

"No. You're right," Kimiko says. "I can't hide forever. I know I must face my fate."

"What does that even mean?" I say. But Kimiko pushes past me to the door. Our conversation is clearly over.

"No," I say. "Don't walk away!" But she does.

"You know why you don't have any friends?" I hiss as she opens the door. "It's not because you're half-kitsune, Kimiko. It's because you're scared."

"I'm not scared!" she says indignantly.

"Yes," I say through clenched teeth. "You are. You're scared of making mistakes, so you keep people away."

"It's different for me! I told you that already!"

"Not that different," I say. "Human beings make mistakes all the time. We call it screwing up! It's what *makes* us human!"

She pushes aside the curtains and slips through the door, her white nightgown billowing out behind her like a cloud, and I'm left alone on the balcony, squinting into the dark.

I lean over the railing, my hair whipping around my face in the wind. I stare out at nothing, just an inky darkness as far as the eye can see. Which is why it's so easy to see the pair of yellow eyes staring up at me from the ground below.

Chapter Eighteen

❧

I WAKE UP AT DAWN. The beach is desolate. There are only a few gulls at the waterline pecking at whatever goodies the high tide has left behind, and any animal tracks that were made during the night are now long gone.

I tiptoe downstairs and make some tea—the herbal kind that's supposed to relax you—then check for messages on my phone. There are a couple of texts from Max; I guess he found cell service after all. One of his texts is about surfing, and the other is about his sister, Chloe, getting food poisoning from eating a bad fish taco.

There's a message from Izzy, too, with a photo of Poos and Chuck curled up on my bed next to the giraffe stuffy I've had since I was six. It makes me smile, and miss home. But what it makes me most, is angry with my dad all over again. It's hard to believe we're actually going to do this moving thing. Cowichan Bay has been our happy place for as long as I can remember. I really do like Anne; she and Dad seem good for each other, but it's worked out fine the way it is for a while now. Why fix it if it isn't broken? The expression makes me think of Ben back home; it's one of his favourite sayings. I wish he were here right now. He's pretty wise, kind of like Yoda, and probably just as old.

I drink my tea and scroll mindlessly through the photos I have stored on my phone. I stop when I see the one of my mother. It's super old, taken before I was born. In it, she's feeding a baby seal off the end of dock #5. It must have been taken the year they bought our houseboat. She's wearing cut-off shorts and a T-shirt, and her hair is even crazier than mine. My dad is standing behind her with one foot poised in the air just behind her as though he's about to push her into the water. He had lots of hair back then and a really awful moustache. They're both laughing their heads off. It's always been my favourite photo of them.

I look at the photo for a long time and it dawns on me that my dad has way more memories of our home than I do, and for the first time, I wonder if pictures like this are sometimes difficult for him to look at.

⁂

"So, you've lived on Haida Gwaii your whole life?" I ask Peter later on. We've finished cleaning a huge section of the beach and have moved on to another part, one that we had to drive to. The whole cove is so peppered with dirty little white bits of Styrofoam it's difficult to tell what is driftwood and what isn't.

"Mostly," Peter says. "Tlell is my home, but I've spent a lot of time on the mainland as well. Done tons of fieldwork in the woods up and down the coastline. That's how I met Jade." At the mention of her name, Jade looks up from where she's working and gives him a sappy smile.

"What kind of fieldwork?" I ask.

"Well," Peter says, throwing some empty beer cans (not from Japan, from sloppy campers) into a separate bag, "it varies. Census projects, research studies, tagging animals, data analysis, things like that."

"Sounds like work," I say. "Complicated."

"Sometimes it is, but I love it. I can't imagine doing any-thing else."

"What about wolves? Have you ever done any fieldwork with them?"

He smiles broadly. "Some, and I'm hoping to get over to the Great Bear Rainforest next year. Wolves. Kermodes. Big trees. Can't wait!"

"Kermodes? The spirit bears?"

"Yup. Pretty special bears."

I add a few pieces of gnarled plastic into the bag. "Well, I hope you get there."

"Me, too."

"Peter?"

"Mmm?"

"But what about the wolves?"

"What about them?"

"Well, I've heard howling. I mean, since that first night we heard them. They sound so . . . I don't know, sad or something."

"They have lots of different songs," Peter says, "and they all mean something different. They're pretty complex animals."

"Are you afraid of them?"

"Of wolves? Never," Peter says. "Wolves are special messengers. Did you know the Nuu-chah-nulth First Nation, who live on this part of the island, believe that wolves represent family?"

I nod, remembering Marcus saying pretty much the same thing in the diner.

"It kind of makes sense if you think about it," Peter says. "Wolves live in family packs, they support each other, work together. Stuff like that."

"Is there actually such a thing as a lone wolf?"

Peter places both his hands on the small of his back and stretches. He doesn't have a ponytail today, and his straight, dark hair reaches past his shoulders. "Yep."

"But why? Why would a wolf leave its pack?" I think of Sitka, all alone in the woods, so silent and watchful.

"Well, there are a few reasons: an older wolf will sometimes leave a pack if the pair of dominant breeding wolves are too aggressive. Or sometimes a young wolf will strike out on its own in search of its own pack. It's a way of ensuring there isn't any interbreeding down the road."

"Sounds harsh," I say. "So much for family."

"Nature's funny that way," Peter says. "But sometimes a young wolf gets lost—separated from the pack. Then they can get disoriented. It happens from time to time around here, because there are so many islands out there in Clayoquot Sound."

"They swim?"

"All the time."

"So what happens while a wolf is lost?"

"They're pretty vulnerable while they're on their own," Peter says. "And if a lone wolf strays into another wolf pack's territory, it can often end badly. That's why they aren't very vocal when they're loners. They don't want to blow their cover."

I remember the howling that seemed to come from over the water, and the fact that Sitka didn't answer back. Is that why? She's playing it safe?

"Then there's the food issue," Peter says. "A wolf on its own can't bring down a deer by itself. They need to hunt in packs to kill those big ungulates."

The *Ghost Wolf* book said the same thing. "So how do they survive?" I can't shake the image of Sitka's very prominent ribs from my memory.

"They usually end up scavenging, or subsisting on mice and smaller critters. Carrion factors in, too."

"Ew. Gross."

"Yeah, well, a hungry wolf has to do what a hungry wolf has to do."

"But, wouldn't one of the pack wolves come looking for their lost member?"

"Lotta islands around here," Peter says. "It could take a while."

"What about the wolves around here?" I ask. "They're not dangerous, right?"

"There hasn't been a resident pack around here for a while," Peter says. "At least not one that I know of. But you'd be lucky to see a wolf anyway. They're shy animals. It's too bad Hollywood has given them such a bad rap."

"But what if one *was* hanging around here, though?"

Peter rests a hand on my shoulder. "Okay, Hannah. You're obviously freaked out about wolves. Do you think you saw one or something?"

"Maybe." I say this tentatively, unsure of how to read Peter, of whether or not I can confide in him.

"Listen, kid," he says. "I can almost guarantee that you didn't. If you saw anything, it was probably Duke, the old malamute that lives a klick or so away. He's a big old grey sucker, and pretty lazy, too. You don't have to worry about him."

"Yeah," I say. "That's probably what I saw."

We carry our bags to the truck, and Peter chuckles and shakes his head. "You think a lot, don't you?"

"I'm a writer's daughter," I say quickly. "I'm naturally curious."

"Well, yeah, I can see that." He chucks the bags into the bed of the Chevy.

I'm grateful I hear Jade call out from somewhere behind us on the beach. "Hey Peter! Come see this!"

He breaks into a jog. "We're leaving in ten, Red Riding Hood," he says over his shoulder. "Stop stressing about the Big Bad Wolf, okay?"

"Hah!" I call after him. "Sure. No worries."

But worrying seems to be all I'm doing lately.

Chapter Nineteen

A FEW MINUTES BEFORE we have dinner, Norman woofs outside the back door.

Then he barks again, even louder.

When Peter opens the door, Norman bursts into the house, his claws scrabbling across the floor as he makes a beeline for Kimiko in the Big Kahuna. He barks wildly, running awkward laps around the old sofa with the fur on his back all ruffed up.

We've all notice that Norman, usually so mellow, is a different dog around Kimiko. But then, I don't imagine there's a dog alive that would be cool about sharing a house with a fox.

"NORMAN!" Ruth scolds, lunging for his collar. She misses and stumbles, falling against the soft cushions piled at one end of the couch.

When Peter does a flying leap and gets Norman in a head-lock, Kimiko is able to make her getaway. She runs into the pantry room off the kitchen, slamming the door so hard behind her that the windows rattle.

"What has gotten into that dog lately?" Ruth frowns. "He's positively demented! I've never seen him behave like this in all his eight years!"

"He hates Kimiko," Sabrina says with a smile. "He totally wants to chew her face off."

"Don't be ridiculous. Norman wouldn't hurt a fly," Ruth says, but she's still frowning. "Peter? Could you please take him back outside? Maybe he needs to run off a little more steam or something."

"Sure thing." Peter heads for the front door, dragging a reluctant Norman along behind him.

"I'll go tell Kimiko the coast is clear," I say.

Kimiko is standing in front of the old oak wardrobe in the pantry. Her eyes are wild, and both of her hands are resting on her chest as though she's having a full-blown anxiety attack.

"Hey, are you okay?" I ask. It's the first thing I've said to her since our little conversation on the balcony.

She tilts her head and sniffs the air a little. "He knows I'm not human," she says. "I can read him. He's confused by me."

There is a tawny flash behind her. My eyes skim over her

head to the wardrobe directly behind her. Its doors are wide open, and in the full-length mirror on the back panel, I see a fleeting image of my own face. But that's not all! I see Kimiko's reflection as well, only it isn't her dark hair, neatly divided into those eight braids that I see in the dusty mirror, it's cinnamon-coloured fur, and one sharp, black-pointed ear! Kimiko moves away from the wardrobe, and the image in the mirror disappears.

"What?" she says.

"The mirror. I saw your reflection." I point to the wardrobe and she stands in front of it again. Her face—her fox face—stares back at her. She jumps away, slams the door shut, and leans against it as though she's afraid that whatever is inside it, might escape. "You see? You see how impossible it is for me?"

"I get it, Kimiko," I say. "I mean, I did see your shadow on the beach when you ran to the lodge."

"You did?"

I nod.

"I feel like that vampire in that book. You know, the one that could never go out in the sun?"

"I know the one," I say.

"Well, it's no way to live."

Ruth sticks her head in the pantry. "Norman's outside," she says. "You girls okay?"

"Sure," I say. "It's all good." I walk casually back through the kitchen, and Kimiko follows.

A moment later I see Jack perched outside on the concrete birdbath. He's sitting very still with his head slightly cocked to one side, listening for something. I watch him dip his head lower as though eager to catch a sound. When a sudden gust of wind sneaks up behind him and ruffles the feathers on the back of his head, he's concentrating so hard he doesn't even notice.

~⁂~

I am woken by a piercing sound outside that makes me jump—a high-pitched cry like a baby screeching. It sends shivers up my spine. I look across the room, but Sabrina and Kimiko are both motionless.

The scream stays with me. It reminds me of when Dad and I were camping on Hornby Island a couple of years ago, and a dog in the campground killed a rabbit just before the sun came up, right near our tent. It was a horrifying thing to hear, like no sound I'd ever heard before. This is the same sound.

I rush to the window and the minute I turn on my phone light, I see Jack swoosh past with something brown and furry in his talons. Jack is hunting at night? Shouldn't he be roosting?

This is too weird. I pull on my sweats and head down the stairs.

Norman gets up quickly as I step past him on the landing. When he sees our bedroom door is closed, he lies back down again.

I sneak out of the lodge and make my way to the compost shed, mud squelching under my boots. I scan the ground for tracks, but there are none this time, just the recognizable treads of Peter's hiking boots—it was his turn to empty the buckets tonight.

I stop by the Sitka spruce, where I listen and wait. And then there *is* a noise—a faint "yip," followed by a soft whimper, definitely canine. A raven cries out, and the sound rises up and over the gusting wind and the rushing ocean behind me. It's Jack, all right, and he sounds stressed. He's flown over my head and into the woods.

I need to find him. I have a weird feeling in the pit of my stomach; something is up and I'm pretty sure it has to do with Sitka. But I'm not going out there alone. I'm going to need backup, and I know just the person to help.

Seconds later I'm in my room again, where thankfully, Sabrina is snoring like an old man. I nudge Kimiko, and she sits up with a start.

"What?" she whispers.

"I need your help outside."

"Why?"

"I'll tell you in a minute. Please, I think the wolf may be in trouble."

"The Okami? The one you call Sitka?" Kimiko is out of bed and into her clothes in record time, and several moments later we are both outside by the Sitka spruce tree.

"What's going on?" she asks.

"I heard something," I say. "I think Sitka is in trouble."

Once we're soon in the woods, and I remember what Yisella taught me about being in the forest the summer I was twelve. Be aware. Be quiet. Listen. And the quieter I am, the more I hear—things like the faint snapping of twigs off to one side, the moan of the trees overhead, and the chilling call of a nearby barred owl.

Although dawn isn't far off, a heavy fog is rolling in off the sea, and a damp chill settles over us. The fog finds its way through the spaces between the trees, making it hard to see, but I am sure-footed, and let's face it, Kimiko is nocturnal. Nothing wrong with her eyes!

But the deeper into the woods we go, the more I stress about Jack and Sitka. When I lose focus completely, I slip on a cedar root, and slam against the trunk of a big cedar. A protruding knot in the wood jabs me in hard my ribs. I curse under my breath. This was a really bad idea. After all, there isn't a law against ravens flying around before dawn, or hunting baby rabbits for that matter. Maybe Jack does this sort of thing all the time. How would I know? And the yip and whimper I heard could have been from Duke, that old malamute Peter mentioned, that lives nearby. Maybe what I heard wasn't a distress call after all. Maybe it was just Duke, "wanting in."

Get a grip, Hannah.
We keep walking.

Chapter Twenty

I TAKE HOLD OF KIMIKO'S arm, close my eyes and listen. Creaking trees: check. Snapping twigs: check. Freaky sounding owl: check. Frantic raven: check. My eyes snap open. A little "yip." There it is again.

Kimiko sniffs the air. "The Okami."

Then I hear them—howling—from somewhere high over the trees. As soon as it starts, the yipping stops. But there's no question in my mind, those wolves are calling to Sitka. But it stops as quickly as it started, and afterwards, there is only the sound of the wind in the swaying branches overhead.

I stop walking and turn around several times, trying to see my way through the fog. Trying to see *anything*! Where *are* you, Jack?

"This fog is crazy!" I say.

"Just stick close," Kimiko says. "My eyes are okay in this stuff."

But sticking close still doesn't keep me from tripping like an idiot, and the more I trip, the more frustrated I become. Hah, so much for my superior forest skills!

Out of nowhere, a small circle of light, no bigger than a quarter, appears just off the ground near my knees. Within seconds, it's joined by two more, and soon there are ten of them! They give off so much light that I can see a moss-covered log a few feet away from me, beside some maple saplings. I whirl around to face Kimiko.

"Are you doing this?"

She nods, her eyes glowing. "For once my Firefox power is working the way I want it to."

"These are awesome!"

The luminescent circles float weightlessly around us. There has to be at least thirty of them now.

When I hear the heavy *swish, swish* of familiar sounding wings coming through the trees, I breathe a sigh of relief and hold out my arm.

"Took you long enough," I say, as Jack lights on my forearm. He hops up to my shoulder and settles his wings beside him. There is a little fur of some kind in one of his talons—rabbit fur, baby soft and fine. I shudder. It isn't a nice thing to think about, but Jack would have had his reasons for the kill. He is a wild creature, after all.

He clucks at me, bobbing his head up and down, and while most of the time we usually understand each other, this is not one of those times.

He looks sideways at one of the floating orbs as it floats past him. When it is mere inches away from his beak, he makes a little snap at it as though it were a bubble he could burst, but misses. Another one grazes my arm and floats down to the ground where it sizzles and burns out, and jumps off my arm and cuts low through the trees.

"Come on, Kimiko." I grab hold of her arm. "He wants us to follow him."

We clamber over slippery roots, pushing away tangles of ground cover, while the silent, bright trail of lights leads us through the fog.

When we push through a thick stand of young alders, we stop walking. Sitka! She whimpers and presses her body back against a log. There are some tiny remnants of the baby rabbit on the ground in front of her, and the fur around her mouth is tinged with red.

The floating lights circle slowly above us, throwing eerie shadows across the ground, and both Kimiko and Sitka sniff the air.

Then I see that Sitka's leg is caught in an old leg hold trap, one that's attached by a thick chain to a now-fallen tree. The rusty device looks ancient, forgotten, like part of an old trap-line from days gone by.

And Sitka, trapped and vulnerable, looks thinner than ever.

Even so, there is a steadiness in her eyes that tells me even though she's injured, she is not afraid.

"We have to spring that trap," I say. "That's why Jack wanted us to follow him."

"How?" Kimiko says.

"We'll work together."

"I *told* you. My powers are unpredictable," Kimiko says. "Especially for something as big as this, especially for the Okami. If I fail—"

"Who said anything about magic or powers. We're going to do this the old-school way. Between the two of us, we can spring that old trap."

Kimiko quickly composes herself, and nods.

"Jack!" I hiss. "The chain."

Jack hops behind Sitka and picks up part of the chain attached to the trap. He tugs at it a little farther down, trying to pull it out from underneath a branch. The chain finally gives, and I hold my breath while Sitka scuttles up to the log, the rusted trap dragging behind her.

"Okay, Jack? Can you distract her?"

Jack snatches at a tiny piece of the rabbit meat and hops in front of Sitka, but the wolf isn't stupid—she's watching Kimiko's and my every move.

"Shhhhhh," I whisper. "We can help you." I take another step forward, and Sitka's ears twitch back and forth. Jack drops the meat in front of her and she cocks her head to one side as he begins to talk his crazy raven talk. She is totally mesmerized by him—it's as if they are sharing some kind of secret, wild conversation.

When the interchange between them is over, I move forward cautiously and squat beside the old leg hold trap. I resist the urge to stroke Sitka's flank. I can't believe she's allowing me to be this close to her. Whatever Jack "said" to her worked. Still, I don't want to push my luck, and if there's one thing I know, it's that wild animals—Okami or not—should remain wary of humans. Once they lose their fear of us, they put themselves in danger.

"Can you stand on the chain?" I ask Kimiko. "Keep it steady for me?"

Kimiko places both her feet firmly on the slippery chain while resting a hand against a nearby cedar trunk. "Okay," she says. "Ready."

I place my palms flat against the rusted levers that protrude on either side of the trap. Thankfully, the steel jaws aren't snapped all the way shut, but even so, Sitka's leg is trapped—a nasty-looking gash visible on the side of it. One of her toes looks mangled, too—she must have been chewing at it out of frustration—and on closer inspection I'm horrified to see that there isn't much left of it.

Kimiko inches along the chain until the side of her boot presses hard against the trap. I push on the levers but they don't budge. "Come *on*!" I hiss under my breath. I summon all my strength and push down hard, so hard that my arms start to tremble. The trap creaks, and there is a loud snap as the levers let go. I rock backwards, my elbow smacking against the ground, but the pain hardly registers as I see Sitka dart away on three legs. She takes cover in the deeper shadows and licks at her injured leg.

"You did it!" Kimiko says, jumping off the chain.

"*We* did it," I say while scouring the ground for a smooth thick stick. I spy one at the edge of the clearing, pick it up and hold it vertically over the trap. In a rush of adrenaline, I raise it high then smash the end of it down on the pan of the trap. The rusted jaws shudder and snap shut, biting against the wood with a force that jars my hands loose. I pick up the chain and try to break it, but it's no use. It's too thick. So instead, I drag the trap into the bushes and bury it with dirt, wet leaves and whatever else I can find. Good riddance evil trap.

"I hope she'll be okay," Kimiko says.

"She's probably going to lose that toe," I say. "But hopefully neither it, nor that cut on her leg will get infected.

"But what if it does?"

"Try and think positive," I say.

"But—"

"It doesn't do any good to think like that, Kimiko. Come on. We've got to get back. The others will be up soon."

"Jack is very clever," Kimiko says. "He led us straight to her."

"He knew we'd be able to help," I say.

We walk out of the clearing, and thanks to Kimiko's special lights, it isn't long before we find ourselves back on the trail. When we break through the trees to the beach, I see the Artful Elephant through the fog on the point and feel a big surge of relief.

Jack hops along on the sand beside us, confused and fascinated by the hovering lights. He has, after all, had a thing for bright and shiny objects. But when he closes in on one, the bright sphere bounces up and over his head like a child's ball, only to fizzle out altogether. It's an action that leaves him perplexed and hopping around like a maniac.

Kimiko stifles a giggle.

"Hmmmm," I say, smiling. "A trickster messing with another trickster."

One by one, the strange lights flicker and die, and by the time we reach the steps to the lodge, it has begun to spit with rain.

Jack hops around the side of the house, no doubt headed for the cat flap in the pantry door—I'm sure a little shut-eye is in his immediate future.

"Hannah?" Kimiko asks when we have both slipped back into our beds without waking Sabrina.

"Yeah?"

"I'm sorry I've been so awful. You've only been trying to help me."

"It's okay," I say.

"The Okami," Kimiko says. "Do you think she'll be okay?"

"I think so," I say. "She seems determined."

"I wish I knew what her message for me was."

The air hangs between us, dark, heavy and silent. I don't say anything, but I wonder if that little wolf might have a message, not just for Kimiko, but for me as well.

Chapter Twenty-One

❦

"WE WERE TALKING to the water taxi guy in town this morning," Jade says at breakfast. "He said he spotted three wolves this week on Meares Island, and another time on one of the nearby Deadman Islets. Big ones, too."

"Must the source of the howling we heard the night we arrived," Peter says.

"Meares Island?" I look out the window. "That's the big island northwest of Tofino harbour, right? It's kind of behind where we are?"

"That's the one," Jade says. "The old-growth forest there was saved from logging back in 1984; big, big trees on that island. Anyway, Warren—that's the water taxi guy—he said those wolves have been pretty vocal—they've been singing every night."

"Maybe you heard them in your sleep, Hannah," Peter says. "Maybe that's what got you so fired up about wolves the other day."

I look over at Kimiko, who is hanging on Peter's every word. She sprinkles a little brown sugar on her oatmeal, but mostly misses the bowl because she's watching him so intently.

"I think I've seen the Okam . . . a wolf," she says. "I think I saw one in the woods last night."

I shoot her a look at the same time that Sabrina drops her spoon in horror. "Seriously? Bears *and* wolves? All we need now is a cougar to start sniffing around here."

Peter looks at Kimiko and raises an eyebrow. "Hmmmmm. Maybe you and Hannah aren't imagining things. Maybe you saw the same wolf."

"Well, keep it on the down low," Jade says. "The last thing we need are trigger-happy locals heading out into the woods with guns."

"What? Are you kidding?" I push my bowl away, my appetite suddenly gone. "They would shoot it?"

"Well, some people have the wrong perception about wolves. They think culling them is a good thing. They call it 'predator control.'"

"That's horrible!" I say.

"I agree," Jade says.

"You know," Peter says thoughtfully, staring off into space. "Wolf medicine is pretty powerful stuff."

Kimiko puts her spoon down. "Wolf medicine?"

"Yeah. If a wolf appears for you, it might be your spirit animal, and spirit animals carry powerful medicine. It might be trying to tell you something about family. Remember what we talked about, Hannah?"

I go back to stirring my already-stirred oatmeal. Sure, okay. Maybe the Okami's message for Kimiko has something to do with *her* home. That would make sense. But maybe Sitka is including me, too, because *my* home is sure on my mind a lot these days.

When everyone has left the table, Kimiko leans over and whispers, "Do you think the Okami—Sitka—is okay?"

"I'm sure Jack is watching over her."

"I have decided I must leave her something." Kimiko says this very matter-of-factly. "Tonight I will leave her an offering by the Sitka spruce tree. To honour her."

"What kind of an offering?"

"Rice, to honour the rice god, Inari. Inari rules over all Okami and kitsune."

"Will leave *who* some rice?" Sabrina plunks herself back down in her chair to pull on a pair of heavy socks.

Kimiko looks like a deer in the headlights, but I quickly jump in. "Oh, rice for the cat—for Pearl. She has an upset stomach. Kimiko thinks some cooked white rice will settle it."

Sabrina totally buys it. "Yeah, that's what our Rosa, our housekeeper, used to give me when I was sick: the B.R.A.T. diet. Works every time."

"Brat?" Kimiko says, confused.

"Yeah. Bananas, rice, applesauce and toast. It's good for you after you've been puking your guts out."

"Puking?"

"Throwing up! Barfing. Vomiting. *God*!"

I shrug and wipe some toast crumbs off the table into my hand. Kimiko gets up from the table and picks up her oatmeal bowl and mug.

Sabrina gasps. "What," she shrieks at the top of her voice, ". . . is *that*?"

Halfway to the kitchen, Kimiko freezes.

"Oh my God! Is that a . . . a tail?" Sabrina drops her bowl back on the table and points at Kimiko in disbelief. Sure enough, a bushy red tail is sticking out from the top of her jeans, its white tip reaching midway up her back.

Sabrina makes a grab for it, but Kimiko shrieks, ducking sideways.

"What the—" Peter laughs as he tries to get a look at the back of Kimiko. "What *is* that? A fox tail?"

Kimiko's face is ashen, her pleading amber eyes filled with terror. She looks absolutely terrified. This is clearly no laughing matter.

I have to think fast! I hop off my chair and rush toward her, pushing her playfully on her shoulder. The push was harder than I meant it to be, and Kimiko stumbles. "Hah! Good one, Kimiko!" I laugh heartily, nudging her again. "But I thought you said that one was mine!"

She looks puzzled, and I quickly turn to the others. "Duh!

Haven't you guys ever seen these things before? They're, like, the hottest thing in Japan right now."

"Hey, wait a second," Sabrina says. "Is that a Shippo tail? Yeah, I've heard about those things! I read an article in one of my dad's magazines about them."

"Oh, me too!" Jade says. "They're a fashion accessory that can read your brainwaves or something, right? I thought they were still in the prototype phase!"

"Exactly! Right!" I say emphatically. "*Everybody* is wearing them in Japan. It's totally an anime thing!"

Ruth appears, shaking her head. "Well," she says. "I have never heard of such a thing. Mind you, that's not surprising!"

"Come on, let me try it on," Sabrina says, making a lunge for Kimiko. She tries to grab the tail, but Kimiko leaps away like . . . like a fox. She looks at me helplessly, a look of desperation on her face.

Thankfully, Jade saves the day. "Don't, Sabrina. You'll break it!" she says. "It's attached to a heart monitor on your ear or something, right Kimiko?"

Sabrina raises her hand to push aside one of Kimiko's braids, but I grab hold of her wrist. "No! Don't touch it! Those monitor things are super delicate!"

Sabrina yanks her hand out of mine. "Whatever, Hannah."

"Well, fox tail or no fox tail, we all need to get to work," Peter says, pulling his toque on.

"Okay. I'll go and put this away," Kimiko says as she nervously pats the end of her tail. "I . . . I'll be back in a minute."

"Well, hurry up," Peter says. "You snooze, you lose!"

Kimiko runs up the stairs, her tail billowing out behind her. What would have happened if *all* her tails had showed up? I dash up after her, but she whirls around and holds out her hands to stop me on the stairs. Her cheeks are streaked with tears.

"Do you finally get it now, Hannah?" she hisses. "Surely you see how useless I am? And this is so typical. I can't even hide my tails! Just when I think I might be able to live an almost normal life, something stupid like this happens!"

"But it's not that big a deal," I assure her. "And it turned out okay in the end! They totally bought the Shippo tail story."

"Thanks to you. If you hadn't been there, I don't know how I would have explained it."

"But I *was* there, so it doesn't matter."

"Of course it matters! I can't expect other people to bail me out every time my powers backfire."

"You're over-thinking things," I tell her.

"I'm not lucky. I'm nothing but a burden. I've known it all my life. This little incident with my tail is just a sign of what lies ahead for me."

"Listen," I say, grabbing her by the shoulders. "You've got to stop feeling so hopeless, okay? Focus on the positive stuff, Kimiko. Like, if you hadn't whipped up those lights last night, we'd still be stumbling around in all that fog."

But she's not listening. She runs up the stairs to our bedroom and before she shuts the door behind her, says. "I'm not working today. Please tell the others I'm not feeling well."

The door slams, and I'm left standing on the landing, frustrated beyond belief. When I turn to go back downstairs, Norman waiting at the bottom, his hackles raised.

Chapter Twenty-Two

WOW. WHAT I WOULDN'T give for just a regular Cowichan Bay sort of day, one where I visit Nell before the bakery opens, to help myself to a warm onion bagel. One where I hang out with Riley on the *Tzinquaw*, or maybe help Ben pull up his crab traps, or spend a rainy afternoon at the Salish Sea Studio, carding wool with Ramona and whoever else happens to drop by. Someone *always* drops by.

Kimiko stays locked in her room all day, claiming to be sick to her stomach. I try on two occasions to talk to her—I even bring her up some peppermint tea—but she refuses to even look at me.

"What's her problem?" Sabrina says when the rest of us head out to work.

"Sick," I say.

Sabrina snorts. "Yeah, right. More like lazy."

You should talk!

Peter and Jade take us through the woods for a bit, and eventually we reach a rugged tucked-away cove. I start working on a mound of tumbled driftwood, pulling plastic and garbage out from between the cracks. I also spend a lot of time staring out at Wickinninish Island. The ocean is choppy today, and I wonder how wolves manage to keep their heads above water swimming between these islands.

All day long I listen for the Meares Island wolves—the ones that Warren, the water taxi guy, said he saw. But all I hear is Jack and some other ravens out on the point, all of them dancing around what looks to be a dead fish. I'm glad he's made some friends, even though it's pretty obvious that ravens aren't big on sharing.

Later on, after all the evening chores have been done, I wander into the kitchen and peek out the back door. Just in case, because while I may be worried about Kimiko, I'm also worried about Sitka's bad leg. She's already so thin. If she's going to be lame as well, finding food will be even harder for her.

The phone on the wall rings, surprising Pearl, who scoots across the floor and down the hall. It's so unusual to hear a land line ring; the strange ring tone seems so completely foreign to me.

Ruth yells from the other room, where she's wrist deep untangling a basket of yarn. "Could somebody please answer that?"

I pick up the receiver. "The Artful Elephant." I say this in what I hope is a good, "telephone answering" kind of voice.

"Hello. Is this Ruth?" a woman asks.

"No, would you like me to get her for you?"

"Well, I'm actually hoping to speak with Sabrina Webber," the voice says. "This is her mother calling."

"Oh, hi, Mrs. Webber," I say. "It's Hannah Anderson. How's Hawaii?"

There is a little hesitation on the line before Sabrina's mom says, "Oh! Hannah. How *are* you? You kids having a great time up there?" She doesn't answer the Hawaii question.

"Yeah," I say. "It's great. Hold on. I'll go and find Sabrina."

Sabrina looks surprised when I tell her that her mom is on the phone. Her cheeks pink up, and she leaps off the couch, making a beeline for the kitchen and slamming the door behind her. But ten minutes later, when I go down the hall to retrieve my laundry from the dryer, I find her sitting alone beside the washing machine.

"What are *you* doing in here?" she says acidly.

"Um . . . getting my laundry?"

She stands up and swipes a hand angrily across her face.

"Are you all right?" I ask.

"Of course I'm all right. Why wouldn't I be all right?"

"Is your mom okay?"

"What's that supposed to mean?"

"It's not supposed to mean anything," I say. "I just thought, you know, if she was calling all the way from Hawaii—"

"Don't even bother," Sabrina says, pushing past me. "What would *you* know about mothers and daughters, anyway?"

The question feels like a punch. "Excuse me?"

"Come on, Hannah. Your mother has been dead for so long she doesn't even count anymore, so just leave me alone, okay?" She bangs the door behind her and stomps off down the hall.

I lean against the wall next to the ironing board, feeling as though I've been slammed in the chest with a cinder block. Everything slows down and becomes surreal. It feels as if I've left my own body, as though I'm looking at my sorry self from somewhere up near the water stain on the ceiling.

I remember this feeling, and I don't like it. I want to come back to myself. I want my limbs to move. I want to get out of this room, only I can't. I feel dizzy and my body feels frozen against the wall.

The phone rings in the kitchen again. It goes on and on and on. Where *is* everybody? Isn't an answering machine going to cut in? When I can't stand it a moment longer, I burst out of the laundry room and answer it.

"Hello?" My voice is thin and reedy.

"Hello? Is that you, Han?" It's not the greatest connection, but I recognize the voice immediately.

"Max?"

"Hey! I got you!" He sounds like his usual enthusiastic self, and hearing him makes me miss him so much. It takes everything I have not to cry.

"Where are you?" I ask.

"In Mexico, Einstein. Remember?"

Remember? How could I forget?

"Hannah?"

I can't open my mouth. I can't say anything because I know that as soon as I do, I'll start blubbering. But Max is on to me.

"Uh-oh. What's wrong?"

I take a gulp of air, and try, unsuccessfully to stifle a sob.

"Come on, Han. Talk."

"Just . . . just a bad day," I say. "Just stuff. Nothing you can do from where you are."

"Is this, by any chance, about moving to Victoria?"

Victoria. It's the icing on this pathetic cake of an evening. I try to answer him, but end up gulping more air instead.

"Aw, Hannah. I'm sorry I'm not there with you."

"It's just that," I stammer, ". . . it's just that everything is happening so fast, Max. Everything is changing, and it feels like I'm not even allowed to have a say."

"Come on. It won't be that bad," Max says. "There are buses to Victoria. And it won't be *that* long before I get my license."

"You don't even have a car, Max."

"But I've saved almost four grand, and that sweet old Volvo is still for sale in the Bay. Red. Standard transmission. Heated seats, even."

I smile, despite myself. Figures Max would have a plan of action in the works, even one for a year or two down the road.

"Are you sure nothing else is bothering you?" he asks.

"It isn't that big a deal," I lie. "It's just, you know. Sabrina can be a real piece of work sometimes. She says things that—"

"Oh, jeez, since when do you care what *she* thinks?"

"I know."

"Let it go, Hannah. We'll both be home soon. And then we'll go do something fun together and eat food that's bad for us."

I smile weakly into the phone. "That would be awesome."

"*You're* awesome," Max says. "Don't forget that."

After I've hung up, the sting of Sabrina's words has subsided a little. Max can always cheer me up, even from a zillion miles away on a white sand beach in Mexico.

Chapter Twenty-Three

I LIE IN BED, waiting to fall asleep, only I don't.

"Kimiko?" I whisper. "Are you awake?" If she is, she's pretending she isn't. Her duvet is pulled up over her head. She is clearly hiding from the world. She wouldn't come down for dinner, and a little while afterwards, Ruth took her up some chicken soup and toast but she didn't touch any of it.

"Kimiko!" I hiss again. Nothing. Eventually, I give up. You can't force a person to talk to you.

I stare at the ceiling. This has been the weirdest spring break ever. I try to stop thinking, and just listen to the sounds I hear around me: Sabrina snoring, Norman's toenails as they clatter on the wood floor outside our door, and a groan in the pipes from somewhere downstairs. Outside, I hear wind, as well as faint rumblings of thunder off in the distance, something that doesn't happen too often on the West Coast.

I breathe in and out, in and out, and concentrate on the ticking of the old grandfather clock in the hall, but each passing second feels more like a passing minute. Sabrina snorts herself awake, turns over and falls back to sleep again. How is that even possible? How can a person say something so cruel and heartless, and then sleep like a baby? Kimiko may only be half human, but sometimes I wonder if Sabrina Webber has a beating heart at all. I squeeze my eyes shut, trying desperately to forget the caustic bite of her words.

Your mother has been dead so long she doesn't even count anymore.

It doesn't work, and the sting returns.

I sit up, and pull my sweatshirt on over my T-shirt, then reach over the side of my bed for my Cowichan sweater. I have to get out of here. It's not that I really care what Sabrina thinks about me, or anyone else for that matter. It's just that hearing her talk about my mom as though she never even existed fills me with an indescribable ache. She died when I was ten but I still miss her everyday. The thing is, lately I can't always remember her that well, things like the details of her face or the tone of her voice. That scares me. Will there come a time when I don't remember her at all?

I need some fresh air. The longer I stay up here in the dark, the more depressed I feel. I find my jeans, pull them on, and tiptoe carefully across the floor and down the flight of stairs.

When I step outside, I hear an odd "pattering" noise up on the roof. I look up but don't see anything unusual. It's probably just Pearl prowling around the way cats do at night.

A blast of wind smacks me in the face when I reach the bottom of the stairs. I raise my chin and let the cold snap of air blow the proverbial cobwebs out of my head. Clutching the collar of my sweater at my throat, I make my way toward the compost shed, hoping that with any luck that I might see Sitka. What I see instead, at the base of the spruce tree, is a small white porcelain bowl of cooked white rice, carefully placed on a flattened mat of sword fern fronds. Seeing it there gives me some hope. Kimiko can't have given up completely if she's left an offering for Inari

I back away from the spruce as the wind tosses the treetops back and forth above my head. I can't imagine any creatures being out and about on such a wild night. I steel myself against the repeated blasts, and head around to the front of the lodge to sit on the bottom step of the deck. I shiver—the wind is getting stronger, and I feel so alone. Now more than ever, I want to be hanging out on dock #5, laughing at Jack while he dive-bombs Poos and Chuck on the deck of our houseboat.

And then, as though he's read my mind, he's beside me, wet, windblown and bedraggled.

"Jack!"

He hops onto my lap, carefully settles his wings and gives his head a couple of shakes. That's when I see he has something in his beak. I lean back a little, allowing the dim porch light to shine down on him. A moment later he drops a curling spiral of lemon rind into my open palm.

It hits me like a bolt from the blue. Lemons. There can only be one reason why he's brought me this. Mom. And in this very moment I remember her as though she's been hanging out with me all day. Suddenly, everything about her is crystal clear: the way she would throw back her head and laugh, and not even be embarrassed when she'd let loose with a giant snort. Or the way she'd manically tap a pencil on the table when she was concentrating—a habit that used to drive Dad and me crazy. But most of all I remember the way she smelled. The lemon oil that she wore every single day for as long as I can remember.

I hold the rind up to my nose, and breathe deep of the fresh citrusy scent. "Thank you, Jack," I say, smoothing down the wet feathers on the top of his head. "Your timing is perfect."

Satisfied, he settles further into my lap, and I wrap my woolly arms around him, blocking out as much wind as I can. Kimiko may be a spirit fox, and Sabrina may be tactless and unkind, but Jack seems to know what I need at the exact moment when I need it. And even though my whole world seems to be changing, it's comforting to know that Jack is just Jack.

"Hang in there, buddy," I tell him softly. "We'll be back in the Bay soon. Back with Riley and Ben, and the Salty Dog Café."

We sit together like this for a long time, staring out toward the sea, where the waves have begun to hammer the shore-line.

"Come on, bird," I say. "It's nuts out here. You better sleep in the pantry again, where it's dry."

I stand up, carefully cradling him in my coat, and he doesn't even try to squirm free.

"This night isn't fit for man or beast," I tell him.

But as I reach for the door of the lodge, Jack suddenly shifts and bursts from my arms. A second later, he is gone, and all I hear is his manic cry as he cuts through the thick night air toward the beach.

I lose my footing on the bottom step and stumble, then race after him through the brush to the beach, shielding my eyes from the building wind and salt spray that assaults me from every direction.

I can hear him—he's close—but I can't see him. I can't see anything! And then, in the middle of the inky darkness, I see a light. Faintly at first, but as I inch my way across the sand, it grows brighter.

When I am only ten feet from the light, I stop. I can't believe what I'm seeing. A russet-coloured fox, one with many tails, is walking in a wide arc near the water. Kimiko! A tiny circle of bright light—her *hoshi no tama*—is carefully cradled in her bushiest tail and held high over her back.

She cautiously watches both of us with her topaz eyes, but she doesn't stop walking the circle. Light from the *hoshi no tama* illuminates the wet tracks her paws leave in the sand.

And then, rising over the sounds of the building storm, I hear it: howling, from somewhere out over the sea. The sound hangs in the darkness, and sends shivers down my spine.

Something moves high up on the beach—a flash of silver! And then a lanky form stands motionless on a rocky ledge, her head raised to the sky, ears pricked. It's Sitka. But she doesn't answer the call from over the water. Instead, she lopes along the rocks, favouring her back leg, before slipping silently back into the forest.

Jack cries out and when I turn back, the fox is gone. Kimiko has simply vanished.

"Kimiko!" I yell into the wind, but nothing comes back. And then there is a crack of lightning, and the sky lights up overhead, and in that brief moment, I see her standing on the same ledge of rock: Kimiko, in her human form. The ledge juts dangerously out over a boiling sea and Kimiko's slender form stands poised at the rock's edge, like a figurehead at the prow of a ship. I watch as she raises her arm over her head, the *hoshi no tama* of light in her open hand.

"KIMIKO!" I scrabble over the rocks and driftwood on the beach to get to her. Another crack of lightning strikes out over the sea—its flash so bright I see Jack soar past, caught hard on a gust of wind.

He reaches Kimiko before I do, but he won't let me out on the slippery rocks. He flies at me shrieking, dive-bombing my head, and flapping his strong wings aggressively in my face. It's horrible!

"Jack!" I shout. "Stop it!"

Kimiko holds up her free hand. "Get away, Hannah. Go back!"

"No!" I shout. "Get away from there! It's too dangerous." The sea churns below us, and a dark angry wave explodes against the rocks, drenching all of us. All those lectures we've had about rogue waves, they're true! Kimiko is asking for trouble out here. This is total lunacy!

I manage to sidestep around the hovering Jack, and make a lunge for Kimiko's free arm. She fixes me with a fierce stare that is half hatred and half fear. Then, without any warning at all, she launches her *hoshi no tama* high up into the air. It hovers for a moment in a kind of slow motion golden haze, before hurtling into the turbulent ocean.

Struggling against the wind, Jack makes a dive for it, but it's too late. It hits the water with a "hiss" and the glow disappears as it sinks down into the inky darkness.

"WHAT DID YOU DO?" I pull Kimiko across the rocks, ignoring her pleas to let her go. She trips, but I drag her off the rocks and finally up onto the beach.

"Are you crazy?" I shout. "You could have been killed! We *all* could have been killed!"

She slumps down on a piece of driftwood, silent and exhausted.

"Seriously? You were going to jump? What if Jack and I hadn't seen you, Kimiko? What if we hadn't been there tonight?" I look over my shoulder to see the shadow of Jack dipping and diving, dodging the wind and rolling waves as he desperately tries to spot the *hoshi no tama*. I want to tell him to stop. It isn't safe out there. But it wouldn't do any good. Jack won't stop until he wants to.

"I wasn't going to jump," Kimiko says, "I just wanted to destroy it! I can't take it anymore! You won't *ever* understand what it's like to be this way. I'd rather stay in the limbo state like before, when I was without my star ball, half alive."

"But don't you realize what you've done?" I'm so angry! I shake her small frame with both of my hands. I can't help it. I can barely spit out the words. "It isn't just about losing your *hoshi no tama*. What if it breaks out there in the surf? If it breaks, you could . . ."

I can't finish. I can't say the words, but Kimiko says them for me. "I know. I could die."

We look at each other in the dark, standing there on the beach in the crazy wind, while white flashes of sheet lightning surround as though we're in the middle of some crazy light show.

"No," I say firmly. "It's *not* broken. Jack *will* find it. You are *not* going to die." I put my arm around her shoulders and walk her up the beach toward the lodge. "You've got to give things a chance. I can help you. And what about the Okami's message for you? You can't just ignore her. You've come this far! You have to try, Kimiko. You can't just give up!"

She shakes her head but doesn't answer.

I look into the wind, trying to locate Jack. It starts to rain, and then it starts to pour! So much, that it's difficult to see five feet in front of me. But Jack is out there. I know it. And I know he won't rest until he finds Kimiko's *hoshi no tama*.

Please. Don't let it be broken. Don't let it be broken.

"Come on," I say gently. "Let's go inside. It'll be okay. Let's just go inside where it's safer."

Kimiko is drenched and shivering, her wet braids hanging down past her waist.

We walk back toward the Elephant in the dark, and halfway there I skid on some slippery rocks, and fall, smashing my knee against a cluster of barnacles.

"Ahh!" I moan, clutching at my knee. I squeeze my eyes shut, grimacing with pain, but when I reach out my hand for Kimiko's, it isn't there. Kimiko is gone!

I can't believe it! *I'm* the one who should have been paying closer attention! How could she just disappear like that? I turn around in circles, but it seems like everything has been swallowed up by the rain and wind. It's impossible to see *anything*.

"KIMIKO!" I run blindly into the dark. I can hear her running toward the trees, sure and quick.

Don't panic. Don't panic. Don't panic.

I say the words over and over again as I run up to the boardwalk. *Don't panic. Stay calm. Tell the others. Don't panic.* If Kimiko's *hoshi no tama* can survive a tsunami—if it can cross the Pacific Ocean and remain intact—then it will soon find its way back to the shore again. It's *not* going to break, not after almost nine hundred years. It's *going* to show up. Jack will see to that.

I push thoughts of the star ball from my mind, trusting that Jack has got it covered. My job is to find Kimiko, and I've got to find her now.

I race to the lodge with my plan in place.

Chapter Twenty-Four

I OPEN THE BACK DOOR but it shudders against the hammering wind, and I have to work hard to steady the rattling doorknob in my hands.

Okay, first things first. I tiptoe up the stairs to our room, and gently push open the door. Sabrina is still sound asleep. I go back out to the hall, open the linen cupboard, and grab a bunch of pillows. Then I creep back into our room and quickly sculpt two "believable" bodies—one under Kimiko's duvet, and one under mine. I know, it's totally a cliché move, but it's worth a shot.

I check my phone. No one will be up for hours. I'll find Kimiko in time. I *have* to!

I grab my Cowichan sweater and tiptoe back downstairs.

Of course, one of the steps creaks loudly on the way down, and I freeze, waiting for a door to open, or for Norman to bark. Thankfully, neither happens. I find the kitchen's junk drawer, and lucky for me, there are two flashlights inside it.

"Don't blow this for me," I whisper to Norman, who is curled up in the Big Kahuna. He raises his head and whimpers a little, but I put my index finger to my lips to shush him, promising to feed him all sorts of "not-allowed" things when I get back. He drops his head on his paws and looks at me with his big, soft eyes. I hate it when dogs do that. It makes me feel like an ogre.

Outside, the raindrops are the size of marbles. An old blue tarp—probably from the woodpile—sails past me, a length of frayed rope whipping out behind it. I brace myself, pull my toque down, and march toward the trees.

The flashlight isn't much good, and I begin imagining all sorts of things I can't see. Things like bears and cougars—cougars that will drop on the back of your neck from high up in a tree. I heard that on a nature show on TV. One bite and you're as good as dead.

I walk straight into the trees anyway, ignoring the mud that finds its way into a hole in my boot. Instantly, my foot is cold *and* wet.

I hear a raven cry, but it isn't Jack. I know his calls by heart. Where *is* he anyway? This storm feels like it's building to be an epic one, but I know he won't rest until he's found the *hoshi no tama*. Jack has never been a quitter.

There are footprints at the edge of the trail. Someone was

here. Small feet, but the prints can't be that old because the rain hasn't filled them up yet. You can still see the tread on the boots. Kimiko. No one else would be out here in this. But her tracks aren't the only ones I see. There is another set, only feet away from hers. I recognize the prints immediately: canine. Wolf tracks—Sitka's tracks.

I follow the tracks, my flashlight aimed at the ground, as they veer off down a narrow deer trail. It grows narrower still, before disappearing completely. I end up blindly bushwhacking through the tangle of underbrush, trying hard to pick up the trail again. What happened to my woods sense, my internal compass, and all the things I learned about the forest from Yisella?

I feel panic rising inside me, and remember how dangerous it is to be in a situation like this without a clear head—a recipe for disaster. So I take a moment and stand completely still, while I try hard to quiet my racing thoughts.

I hear a tiny whimper, and my head shoots up. I make my way through the dripping foliage toward the sound, ignoring the wet smack of branches against my cheek. Something is on the ground, near a clump of salal by some exposed bedrock. I aim my flashlight at the shape, and beside her, curled against her back, is Sitka, her sweeping tail wrapped over Kimiko's torso.

I don't dare move. Sitka raises her head, fixes me with a stare and sniffs the air.

"Easy," I whisper, more to myself than to Sitka. The three

of us are frozen, each eyeing up the other, unsure of what to do next.

"Kimiko?" I whisper. She's soaked through and white as a ghost.

"Are you okay? You're shivering so hard! Can you get up?"

"I . . ." she mumbles. "Just . . . leave . . . me . . . here." Sitka sits up too, and favours her back leg. I can see that the cut is still there, but the mangled toe isn't! All that remains is some matted bloody fur where Sitka's toe used to be.

"The Okami," Kimiko says. "She stayed with me."

"You see?" I say. "She's looking out for you, Kimiko. But still, you're going to get hypothermia if we don't get you back to the lodge."

"No. Just leave me here." She struggles to get up, but becomes suddenly uncoordinated and sinks back down on the ground.

I reach over and try to pull her onto her feet. In a flash, Sitka is up on all fours and has limped away from me.

"Let go," Kimiko insists, but she can't shake me loose.

"Kimiko," I say calmly, "you can't just stay out here. Think about what you're doing! How do you think all this will go over? If you disappear, or anything bad happens to you, Ruth is going to have to take the fall. Her business will be ruined. How can you do that to her?"

"I have to think about what is best for me."

"Cut it out," I say, angry now. "You've been messed up ever since Sabrina saw your tail. You—"

"This isn't about my stupid tail," Kimiko says, frowning. "The tail was nothing. But that incident showed me how completely unsuited I am for mortal life. Don't you get it, Hannah?"

"Stop it! People aren't going to forget that good old Ruth, long time proprietor of the Artful Elephant, let a young girl come to harm in the woods. You really want that on your conscience? She has been so good to all of us. This is how you are going to repay her for being so awesome?"

Eventually, she sighs, gets onto her knees and reaches for my hand. I help her to her feet. She sways a little, and grabs my arm.

"Dizzy?" I ask.

She nods. This isn't a good sign. Clumsiness and dizziness can both be signs of hypothermia, something Aunt Maddie taught me.

"The Okami," Kimiko says, but when we look to the fir tree, Sitka is gone.

A blast of wind threatens to knock us both to the ground, but we hobble through the bush, dodging debris and twigs that twist and sail past us at warp speed. The driving rain is bitterly cold, and the ground has turned into a soggy, foot-sucking quagmire.

Kimiko is running out of steam; she's dragging her feet and keeps falling to her knees every few steps.

"Kimiko!" I plead. "We're almost at the lodge. Come on. Just a little further."

"I . . . I can't," she mutters. "I'm too cold."

But there's no way I'm going to let her give up. Not now, not after everything. I didn't come out here in the middle of the night for a nice, serene nature walk. I didn't come out here to fail!

"TRY HARDER!" I yell over the wind.

She whimpers, but she does tighten her grip on my arm, and steps it up a little.

The rain becomes so heavy it's blinding, and soon walking anywhere is completely futile. And while the flashlight is fully charged, it hardly does any good at all.

"Kimiko," I say. "We need those hovering lights again. Brighter ones."

"I can't. I don't have my *hoshi no tama*. I don't have any powers at all."

Duh! Of course! But Jack will find it. And then he'll bring it to us. He's probably on his way right at this very moment.

I duck under a spruce tree, steadying Kimiko against its wide trunk. "We have to get out of this rain for a bit. We have to get you warm."

"Okay," she says, but I wonder if she has even understood me. It's as if she's fading in and out, as though she's trying not to fall asleep.

I wipe water from my face, and see a thick copse of trees that looks promising—a place where we can take shelter for a while. Kimiko's braids are pushed back, and her small pointed ears twitch back and forth a mile a minute.

Chapter Twenty-Five

SOMEHOW, I MANAGE to find a few bits of dry bark and wood shavings, and luckily, have a box of wooden matches tucked away in a hidden pocket inside my sweater. I get a flame going pretty quickly, and soon the air fills up with the smell of smoke and wet wool.

I take off my Cowichan sweater and wrap it around Kimiko. It's wet, but it's real wool, so it will help to keep her warm. Soon the fire is throwing off some real heat.

Then, through the crackle of flames and wind in the forest, I hear it—the wolves—their song floats high over the forest from somewhere far away, then weaves in and out of the trees to settle around us by the fire. I look over at Kimiko, but she just stares like a zombie at the flickering light. When I scan the perimeter of the clearing for Sitka, there is no sign of her.

"Sitka," I say. "The Okami. I saw her tracks earlier. She was following you."

Kimiko raises her head in the wind. "I don't smell her anymore. But without my *hoshi no tama*, I don't smell much of anything."

"Are you feeling warmer yet?"

She nods, even though she is still shivering.

"Here." I take a half-eaten chocolate chip granola bar from the pocket of my sweater and hand it to her. "It isn't much, but it's something."

She accepts it gratefully, and finishes it in two bites.

When the fire begins to sputter, I stamp it out and cover the few remaining sparks with wet earth. I get Kimiko up on her feet, and keep a firm hold on her as we start down a narrow single-track trail through the trees. She is light as a feather. There's nothing to her at all. We keep going until we reach a boggy clearing, flanked on both sides with the first tiny spring shoots of vanilla leaf.

"The trail is washed out here," I say, stopping abruptly, but we're already soaked to the bone. We wade through water that reaches halfway to our knees. The cold stings my toes and the soles of my feet, but I am determined to break out of the woods and get Kimiko back to safety.

Finally, about the same time that my toes become numb, the black night surrounding us begins to loosen its grip and the wind suddenly drops. We begin to be able to make out the dark shapes of the trees and bushes against a gradually lightening sky. Knowing that daybreak is close gives me extra energy, despite the steady rain that continues to fall.

The air begins filling up with familiar and reassuring sounds: seagulls crying out, the occasional scree of a bald eagle, the first hopeful "*rbbbbiittts*" of a few brave frogs as they emerge from their long winter sleep in the mud. But there are no raven cries, and from out of nowhere, a shiver runs through me, one that has nothing to do with the state of my feet or the wet chill in my bones.

The hairs stand up on the back of my neck. Something feels wrong.

Very wrong.

"Why did you stop?" Kimiko asks as I stand still on the trail.

"Something isn't right," I say frantically. "We have to hurry."

But hurrying is easier said than done. My heart thumps harder and harder as I struggle to support Kimiko along the soggy, root-covered trail. With every step I take, more fear builds inside of me. I've got to get out of here! I've got to get to the beach!

"It's okay," Kimiko says as she slams awkwardly into my shoulder. "Let go of me. I can walk by myself. Really."

And then I see a sliver of ocean between the thick trunks of cedar trees.

Without another word, I leave Kimiko and run ahead. I push through the tangle of undergrowth and burst onto the rain-soaked sand. The sea air stings my tired, smoke-burned eyes, but it's getting lighter—I can see the Artful Elephant up the beach, weak curls of smoke rising from the chimney, remnants of last night's fire in the Big Kahuna.

Giant pieces of driftwood have been upended all along the beach, and broken fir, spruce and cedar boughs lie scattered every which way—some of them the size of small trees.

Oddly enough, the ocean is now calm, and laps gently at the tangled kelp and other seaweed that has collected at the tide line. But there is something at the water's edge that looks out of place. Something black. The closer I get, the more my legs feel as though they're sinking into quicksand. The black shape begins to look familiar. My pulse quickens and thuds in my ears. Then I see his feathers, the curve of his beak, and I stop moving. I freeze. This can't be happening. This has to be part of a cruel and twisted dream. It won't last. I'm going to wake up any minute and find myself at home on our houseboat. I'll smell the coffee brewing downstairs in the kitchen. I'll hear Dad humming, just like always.

No, no, no, no. NO!

But I'm not waking up. The morning light spills over the sand, highlighting what I already know to be true. But I still can't move. Time stops, and I put my hand over my mouth, afraid I might throw up. It's like the wind has been knocked out of me and its punch has left another hole inside me—a hole as deep and hollow as the one left there the day my mother died.

I ball up my fists at my sides, and squeeze my eyes shut, wanting to turn and run back into the woods. But I can't abandon him. I have to go.

The last fifty feet are the hardest steps I have ever taken. I don't know how my legs carry me to the tide line but they do. I force myself to look down at the sand and when I do, my heart breaks.

Chapter Twenty-Six

THERE ARE NO WORDS. Only pictures. A slide show of the past three years: slides of Jack, my best friend. The images cycle through my head like a badly edited movie: Jack outside the Toad-in-the-Hole Bakery, looking for crumbs; Jack, never quite mustering the courage to hang out with Sadie, Ben's overconfident African grey parrot; Jack the hero, who helped to bust the poaching ring last summer; Jack, and his multitude of crazy calls. His impatience when he wanted my attention—his cocky swagger as he strutted along dock #5, looking for scraps. Looking for me.

Jack. My Jack.

He lies lifeless at my feet, the water slapping against his wet, blue-black feathers. Each wave pushes him a little, and then pulls him back as it retreats. There is a twist of seaweed around one of his legs, and when I push it aside, my eyes are so full of tears that at first I miss the faint light that glows through the dark green fronds. I wipe at my face and there it is—Kimiko's star ball—her *hoshi no tama*. The twisted and knotted chain is wrapped tightly around both of Jack's legs. And then I understand. He must have found the star ball, but the storm. The wind. He must have been unable to get back to shore in time. And then the chain . . .

I lean over him. He is so cold, so still. His eyes are squeezed shut as though he's sleeping, and his head is partially hidden by one of his wings.

When I rest my cheek against him, the pain I feel is worse than anything I could ever imagine. I sit back on my knees, and with shaking hands, pick him up and hold him close against my heart. I wrap my arms so tightly around him but I know it isn't any good. It's too late. It's just too late.

Somehow, I find my way to my feet. I stay at the waterline for a moment, cradling Jack, staring zombie-like out at the ocean. I've lived by the sea my whole life. I miss it so much when I'm away from it, but everything is different now. Now what I see is an ocean that I hate. How can it be so calm and peaceful now, yet just hours ago so violent and menacing? How could it have been so cruel? How could it take away my best friend in the world?

I walk on heavy legs up the beach and find shelter in between a haphazard pile of driftwood. Despite my shivering, I peel off my sweatshirt—down now to just my T-shirt—and lay it on the smooth sand. I place Jack on it, and go to work on the star ball, carefully untangling the chain from around his legs until it the ball rolls away onto the sand, the glowing light flickering weakly inside it. I glare at the *hoshi no tama*, wishing now that I'd never found it. Wishing now, that I'd never come here.

I don't know how to do this. I don't know how to go on without Jack. How can he be gone? I clutch at my sides, feeling dizzy, and then feel a hand on my shoulder. Peter.

"Hannah," he says softly, squatting down beside me. He puts his hand over mine, the one that's resting on Jack. "I was getting wood. I saw you from the woodpile. Hannah, I'm so sorry."

I look up into his eyes, so warm and caring, but I can't even open my mouth. There just are no words. None.

"How," he says softly. "How did this happen? What happened?"

"He . . ." I stammer. "He must have drowned. His legs . . . they got tangled in that necklace. In the storm."

Peter doesn't ask any more questions. He just keeps his hand over mine while I cry, and drapes his jacket around my shivering shoulders.

My teeth won't stop chattering, and I feel exhausted. I drop my head and press my fingers against my temples, squeezing my eyes shut. But even with my eyes closed, the image of Jack remains.

"Hannah." Kimiko, her face contorted with fear, stands beside me.

"NO!" A rush of adrenaline surges through me as I jump to my feet and shove her away. "GET AWAY FROM HIM!" I yell, pushing Kimiko aside. She falls over like a feather. There is no weight to her at all. But I know what she's after; she's changed her mind. She wants her power back after all. She doesn't care about Jack or me, or anyone except herself. All she wants is her *hoshi no tama*.

"THIS IS ALL YOUR FAULT!" I sob. "*You're* the reason that Jack is dead! You're the reason for everything that has gone wrong up here! I can't believe I tried to help you!"

"Hannah, calm down." Peter pulls me off her and I crumple on the sand.

"I'm sorry, Hannah," Kimiko whispers in a small voice, and then, still shivering, but summoning up all her strength, she snatches the star ball from where it sits in the sand. She holds it high over her head and brings it down hard on a rock at her side. The glass explodes into shards. The bright light bursts forth, and Kimiko catches it and holds it in her hands. When she leans over Jack, I make a lunge for her, but Peter grabs hold of my shoulders.

"Let me go, Peter!" I scream. "Get her away from Jack!"

Kimiko opens up her palms and the golden light—so much brighter now—escapes her hands to wash over Jack on the ground. His entire body becomes infused with light, almost as though he is on fire. It's more than I can bear! I wrench myself free of Peter, shove Kimiko aside and reach out for Jack. But I can't touch him. It's as though the light has created a vibrating force field around him. All I can do is watch helplessly as he starts pulsating with a kind of blinding electricity.

"WHAT HAVE YOU DONE?" I screech at Kimiko.

But Kimiko can't answer me. She slumps down heavily on the sand, exhausted. The light that envelopes Jack begins to flicker and fade, and a minute later, it disappears altogether.

Peter looks stunned. "What the—"

We stare at Jack, watching in disbelief as his black feathers begin to change. His dark wingtips become tinged with white at the edges. His tail feathers begin turn from black to grey and then lighter still.

"What's happening to him?" I cry, clutching Peter's arm. I watch as each one of Jack's feathers, once so glossy and black, turn pearly snow white, right before my eyes. It happens in a matter of seconds. Even his beak, legs and talons change from their usual black to a light, pinkish hue.

"Peter!"

"I know!"

When the transformation is complete, one of Jack's wings stirs. Just a little. A second later his leg twitches. And then his whole body shudders and jerks from side to side as both of his wings slowly unfurl. He eyes—once black, now blue— blink several times before looking straight into mine.

"JACK!" I drop to my knees and stretch my arms out in front of me, and then, just like always, he cocks his head to one side, gets up and hops forward. He lets out a little croak and steps tentatively onto my forearm, digging those strong and familiar talons straight through my sleeve and against the flesh of my arm.

"It's you! You're back! You're here!" I can barely contain myself. Jack is alive! He's right here! Alive! He picks up a little bit of my wet hair in his beak and gives it a tug, and I laugh out loud. I want to pinch myself but I'm not dreaming. Jack is right here!

"Holy crap!" Peter says, looking a little pale. "I do not believe what just went down."

"Me either!" I say, "But look! Peter, Jack is—"

Kimiko sits on the wet sand, pale and silent.

"Kimiko!" I say incredulously. "How? How did you do—"

"What," a voice says beside me, "is *that*?" I look over and see Sabrina, the crocheted afghan from the couch draped around her, and her hair sticking up every which way. "I just got up. I could see you guys from the kitchen window."

"It's Jack," I say quietly.

Sabrina stares at Jack as though he has six heads. "Yeah, right," she says. "Like I'm supposed to believe that's your raven friend? As if."

At that precise moment, Jack caws and flaps off my arm to land right on top of my head.

"OW!" I say, shooing him off and back onto my arm. "Cut it out, Jack."

"Wait. Is this for real?" Sabrina says. Then she stops looking at Jack, and starts staring at Kimiko and me. "Why are you guys so wet? Did you fall in the ocean or something?"

"Yeah," I say. "We did. Over there." I point to a little rocky point down the beach.

"Which is why you both need to get back to the lodge and get warm. And right now," Peter says. "If Ruth catches wind of this, you guys are toast." But despite the warning, he doesn't move; he just stares at Jack and keeps shaking his head.

"Isn't anyone going to tell me what happened?" Sabrina asks impatiently.

"We don't know!" Peter and I say in unison.

As we walk back to the lodge, I hang back a little with Kimiko. "Are you okay?"

"I just need a hot shower," she says quietly. "But I feel a lot better all of a sudden."

Strangely, the colour has returned to her cheeks, and her eyes look brighter.

"But your *hoshi no tama*," I say. "It's broken. What if—"

"I know," she says, "I don't get it either. But I feel okay. Really."

I stop and look out at the ocean, the familiar weight of Jack now on my shoulder. Thanks to Kimiko, Jack is here. I have *so* much to say, but I can't think of the right words. I have felt so many mixed up emotions in the past hour, that I can't make sense of anything. "Kimiko, I—"

She puts an index finger to her lips. "It's okay. We can talk later."

So we just walk, because maybe Kimiko is right. There will be time to talk later.

But almost immediately, I stop suddenly and turn around.

"What is it?" Kimiko asks, her teeth chattering.

"I'm not sure." But through the spitting rain and deep in the shadows between the trees, I'm pretty sure I catch a fleeting glimpse of silver fur.

"Did you see something?"

"Sitka," I say. "I think she's still watching us."

Kimiko and I stand together, motionless on the beach, and wait for our wolf to reappear. When she doesn't, we turn around and walk the rest of the way to the lodge.

I place the palm of my hand over Jack's feet, and he starts pecking at the signet ring on my baby finger—a present my mom gave me when I was seven. I can't begin to describe how wonderful it is to feel the heat radiating off his body.

Inside the Artful Elephant, the clock on the stove is blinking—a clear sign the power was out. No big surprise there.

When Norman spies us, he thumps his thick tail against the side of a kitchen chair, eager for someone to remember that it's his breakfast time. While Peter dumps the kibble into his bowl, I can't help noticing that Norman doesn't seem the least bit bothered about Kimiko. In fact, he barely notices her at all. He's well aware of Jack, though, and Jack is not too stoked about it. I make a beeline for the pantry, shove the woolly afghan into the old forgotten dog crate that sits in the corner, and place Jack inside it. He seems happy to be in a safe place—even thought was once probably Norman's—and settles himself deep into the afghan. With any luck, he will sleep, and I can check on him while he does.

I take a moment to stroke the side of his smooth white head, and stare into his familiar eyes. They have a light blue-grey hue to them now, but they're still Jack's eyes. They still look at me with the same mixture of familiarity and cheekiness. "Go to sleep, buddy," I tell him. "You've earned it."

Peter puts the kettle on while Kimiko and I each take long hot showers up in our room. When Kimiko is done, she looks about one hundred percent better. In fact, she looks better than ever. So much for the hypothermia I thought she had. I, on the other hand, look like a tired hag!

When we're finally warmed up and dressed in dry clothes, we come downstairs, where Peter hands us mugs of hot, sweet tea. I can't remember when anything has ever tasted so wonderful. "Thanks, Peter," I say. He gives me a wink and a big smile. He doesn't ask me any questions about why Kimiko and I were outside in the first place. I'm grateful for that, because I honestly don't know what I'd say, and I wouldn't want to lie to him. Peter is a pretty decent guy.

When I'm confident that Jack is sleeping soundly, I walk to the window in the Big Kahuna. The ocean is flat as a pancake now, the calmest I've seen it since we arrived here. There isn't a puff of wind, and the sky is already bluer than blue. In my whole life, I've never seen weather change so quickly from one extreme to the other.

"That was one powerful storm!" Ruth says, coming down the stairs. "And I overslept! My alarm never went off! Did we lose power?"

"Yep, and we figured we would let you sleep in for once," Jade says. "Apparently there's a big tree down on the main road, too.

"Pretty sure everyone around here lost power," Peter says.

And Kimiko is no exception.

Chapter Twenty-Seven

IT'S GOING TO BE a rough day of work. All I really want to do is sleep for about one hundred hours, but that's just not going to happen, and it isn't like I can tell anyone why I'm so tired!

When I go upstairs to get some dry work gloves, Norman is pacing back and forth outside our bedroom door, wagging his tail.

"Nope. Don't think so, buddy," I say. "Your nemesis is in there." I open the door a few inches, and begin to squeeze my body through, but Norman lets out a resounding "woof" and pushes right past me.

"Hey!" He bounds across the room and launches himself right in the middle of Kimiko's bed.

"OH!" Kimiko jumps, and the notebook she's been writing in bounces off the bed and onto the floor.

I rush to grab Norman's collar, but my hand stops in mid-air, and I can't help but laugh. This crazy black dog has somehow managed to crawl onto Kimiko's lap, his back end wiggling so enthusiastically that the lamp rattles on the bedside table.

Kimiko shuts her eyes tight, and tries unsuccessfully to push him off, but the harder she pushes, the closer Norman gets to her. When he beings covering her face with slobbery wet dog kisses, I decide it's time to intervene. Easier said than done; it's no easy task to hold back eighty pounds of wiggle!

Kimiko wipes at the dog slobber on her cheeks. "Ugh! My face is all sticky."

"Those are dog kisses," I say. "They're always sticky."

"Well, I guess it's not *that* awful," she says, a smile forming.

"This is really strange," I say. "I mean, not only the past twenty-four hours, but this whole Norman thing, too. It's like he's suddenly decided that you're his best friend or something." And at that very moment, he breaks free from my arms and commando crawls up the bed to snuggle close to Kimiko again. Only this time, he buries his snout in her armpit.

"Yep, he's definitely stoked on you," I say.

"I've never been friends with a dog before," she says, her face flushed.

"Well, dogs are awesome. I have a dog friend back home named Quincy. He doesn't smell great, but he's pretty cool."

Kimiko lays a tentative hand upon Norman's head, and then gently rubs him behind his ears. Norman responds by lunging forward to lick her on the end of her nose. I honestly wouldn't believe any of this if I weren't watching it happen right before my eyes. Who *is* this dog?

Kimiko smiles. "I think I like him."

"See? That's how it works. He's totally winning you over."

"Hah," Kimiko says. "Could be." She gets up and goes to the bathroom to wash her face, and that's when I notice there is something different about the way she walks. She seems a little off balance—a little uncertain of her normally sure-footed steps.

"Are you still dizzy?" I ask.

"Maybe a little," she says.

"Well, don't lock the door," I caution as she walks into the bathroom. A moment later she peeks her head around the door, a look of disbelief on her face. "HANNAH! Come see!"

"Come see what?"

"Look!" She points at her reflection in the big mirror over the sink. Only this time, it isn't the face of a fox that stares back. This time, it's a pretty Japanese girl who looks at us—a Japanese girl with eight braids and twinkling amber eyes that flash with excitement.

"It's my reflection!" she says, gripping her hands together. "My human reflection!"

"I see!"

"A kitsune's reflection is *never* a human reflection," she explains. "Even when we're in human form. Mirrors have always been one of my biggest fears!"

She leans over the sink to study her face in the mirror, poking at her cheeks and shoulders as though she half expects to see her image vanish into thin air.

Sabrina comes into our room, and, sidestepping Norman, she walks into the bathroom to stand beside Kimiko. She peers into the mirror, obviously confused about what it everyone is looking at. "What?"

But Kimiko and I can't stop smiling, and nothing either of us can say will make any sense to Sabrina anyway.

"Oh," Sabrina says finally, nodding her head. "I get it now."

"You do?" Kimiko says.

"Sure." Sabrina leans over the sink and stares at Kimiko's reflection closely. "It's plainly obvious. You need to do a better job plucking your eyebrows."

Kimiko and I double over laughing, while Sabrina looks at us as though we've completely lost our minds.

"I don't see what's so funny about sloppy personal hygiene," she says. "But they're your eyebrows." She sneers at both of us. "And FYI," she says, closing the door behind her, "we're supposed to be *working* right now."

What? Since when did Sabrina grow a work ethic?

I check in on Jack in the pantry one more time before I go outside. I find him casually investigating a sack of potatoes, tugging at a few loose strands of the burlap bag as though nothing out of the ordinary ever happened. How can he have this much energy?

"You," I say, folding my arms over my chest, "are something else."

He loses interest in the potatoes, and struts across the floor to check out some acorn squash in a box in the corner, looking at me briefly as me as if to say, "I know."

～✿～

"It doesn't make any sense," Ruth says after lunch. "A bird can't just change its colour. Chameleons, sure, but ravens, I don't think so."

"Well you're looking right at him," I say, watching Jack preen his snowy-white feathers on the concrete birdbath outside.

"It isn't possible," Ruth says. "It must be a different raven."

"He's not an *it*," I say. "He's Jack."

Ruth looks to Peter for backup but Peter is just smiling his wide, easy smile, his arms folded across his chest as he leans against the door frame watching Jack.

"Peter?" Ruth says.

"Mmmmm?"

"Are you buying this stuff?"

"Well, I'm not *not* buying it. You can't always have all the answers, Ruth," he says, his eyes crinkling up at the edges. "Even psychics can't know *everything*."

"So . . . you think that's Jack?"

"Not saying it isn't."

"Come on!"

Peter pushes himself away from the door and plops himself down on the end of the couch in the Big Kahuna. "Back on Haida Gwaii," he says, "there was once a white raven. He lived in Port Clements for a couple of years. I used to see him all the time when I was a kid."

"Seriously?"

"Yep. He was pretty special, and he got pretty chummy with a lot of the local folks in town."

"What happened to him?"

"He flew into a power line in 1997. Electrocuted."

"No way!" I say, "That happened to an eagle back home last year. My friend and I helped raise the eaglets."

"I think it happens more often than you'd think," Peter says. "That raven is in the Port Clements museum now. And the people of Haida Gwaii believe that a white raven returns when light is brought back to the land."

"Light? What kind of light?"

"Not sure, really. Maybe it's more of a metaphor," Peter says. "Light being symbolic for good juju, perhaps."

Like Jack coming back to us, I want to say. If that isn't good juju, I don't know what is.

"So, if the white raven has returned," Kimiko says. "This is a good sign?"

"I would have to say it is," Peter says.

"You know," Sabrina says. "My mom's friend survived this

super awful plane crash ten years ago, and her hair turned white overnight."

"Hah," Jade says. "I think that's totally an urban myth."

"Well, tell that to my mom's friend," Sabrina says. "Anyway, maybe that's what happened to Jack. Maybe something spooked him and his feathers just turned white."

But Peter just smiles.

I watch Jack on the birdbath. He flaps his wings as though he's about to take flight but then changes his mind, holding them out proudly on either side of him like a butterfly. I quickly grab my phone—Jack is practically *begging* to have his picture taken.

⁂

Even though Kimiko and I are mega sleep-deprived, we work steadily together on the beach. It feels wonderful to be warm and dry, after a nice hot breakfast. The sky overhead has become a periwinkle blue, and a cool, refreshing breeze blows in off the water. It's like last night's storm never even happened.

Jack wasn't the only one affected when Kimiko broke her *hoshi no tama*. Back in the diner, Marcus had said a kitsune couldn't survive without its star ball, but he didn't say anything about how a *half-kitsune* might be affected. Kimiko's energy has returned with a vengeance! She runs all over the sand, chasing seagulls and climbing over driftwood. She lobs slimy pieces of sea lettuce at our unsuspecting heads when she thinks we aren't looking, and creates clamshell pictures along flatter pieces of driftwood from one end of the beach to the other. But the most awesome thing of all is the time she spends chasing her own shadow on the sand—her shadow that, up until now, had four legs and multiple bushy tails.

"What's with Kimiko?" Jade asks me during a break. We're both building a sandcastle near the water, although if you ask me, Jade seems more intent on digging a ridiculously deep moat than she is in creating any sort of epic fortress.

"She's just happy," I say. "You know. Sunny day and all that."

"I guess," she says. "But, how old is she, six?"

"Uh . . ." I point to our sandcastle, complete with sand dollar windows and a seaweed grass lawn. "How old are *we*?"

"I see your point," Jade says, because she's like, twenty-five.

But childish or not, we manage to construct an impressive bull kelp bridge over our moat, as well as a few misshapen, slightly tilted turrets.

Sabrina comes up behind us and drops to her knees on the sand. "Can I help?" She picks up a wet handful of sand and slaps it back and forth between her palms.

"You're getting dirty," I say, eyeing her suspiciously.

"It's just a little sand."

Who is this girl, and where did Sabrina go?

"Oh, come on," Sabrina says, rolling her eyes at both of us. "There isn't a person alive who *doesn't* like building sand-castles!"

I shrug. We haven't said much to each other since the whole "mother" comment she made.

Soon Kimiko grows tired of dancing with her shadow and wanders over to see what the three of us are doing. "Here," she says, squatting beside me. "Let me." She puts some broken clamshell detailing on the turret, and I pause to watch Jack on the top of a nearby cedar tree. The sunshine bounces off his bright white wings, and I'm pretty sure he's well aware of just how majestic he looks by the way he holds his head so high and proud. He is truly magnificent. I nudge Kimiko's arm and point to him. She smiles, and nudges me back.

When the break is over and the others have wandered away from the castle, I ask the question that's been on my mind all morning. "Kimiko?"

"Yes?"

"You broke your *hoshi no tama*. But you're fine. *Better* than fine, even. What's going on?"

"Honestly, Hannah . . . I don't know. All I know is that I had to help you. I had to help Jack." Her smile is one of the biggest I've ever seen her make. She nods her head toward Jack in the tree. "He gave his life trying to help me," she says earnestly. "It was my turn to help him."

My eyes grow wet, and I feel as though I may have misunderstood Kimiko all along. I should never have judged her so harshly. Because, what must it have been like to have people scared of you all the time—to live for so long but never feel an authentic connection with anyone? And then, the tsunami . . .

it's a wonder Kimiko has been able to function at all. It makes me feel kind of ashamed, especially when I think about how sour I've been about the upcoming move to Victoria. Kind of a first world problem in the grand scheme of things, I guess.

"So," I say to Kimiko, "do you still feel different?"

"Yes. I do. Different, but wonderful! Everything looks brighter somehow, more alive." She sniffs the air. "And I can't smell anything! Except the sea!"

"And this is a good thing?"

"Before today," she says, spreading her arms wide, "I could smell everything. I could smell people, and the animals in the forest, danger . . . just, everything! But not any more." She sniffs again. "Now I smell only the sea."

"Same here," I say. "But then, I'm only human."

Kimiko laughs out loud. "I think," she says, "we have that in common now."

"Is that even possible?" I say. "That you are fully human now?"

"Well, how else do you explain it? My heightened sense of smell has gone. I have a human reflection, and I cast the most beautiful shadows!"

"And there's Norman, too" I add. "Don't forget him. He's suddenly super stoked on you."

"You see? That would never happen if I were still a kitsune," Kimiko explains.

Before I can answer, a little shrew skitters across the ground, headed for a rotting stump a few feet away from us. Kimiko makes a sudden lunge forward and then stops herself and laughs again.

"What?"

"I feel different, all right. Normally, that shrew would have made a tasty snack. They used to be one of my favourite afternoon munchies."

"Ew! Gross!"

"I know, right? I can't think of anything more disgusting now." Kimiko places her hands on her stomach, as though she's trying to settle it. "You couldn't pay me to eat that shrew now."

"Well, thank goodness for that."

Kimiko raises her face to the sun. "Being human is awesome!"

"I'd have to agree," Peter says, appearing on the beach behind us.

Kimiko blushes, and we both laugh as a wave breaks, destroying one side of our sandcastle.

Chapter Twenty-Eight

⚜

"WELL GUYS," PETER SAYS, snapping his field guide shut. "Your time here is almost over. I'd say we've done a pretty good job of cleaning up the coves around here. What'll we do to wrap things up?" He tosses the book on the coffee table and stretches against the back of his chair in the Big Kahuna.

Norman jumps up onto the couch next to Kimiko and puts his head on her lap. She immediately starts scratching his chin. It's like they've been friends forever.

"Want to go into town?" Jade asks. "I mean, *brownies*, right?"

⚜

Downtown Tofino is busy, full of surfers who come here from all over to catch the big waves. We see their trucks and vans parked everywhere, the big colourful boards strapped to roof racks or sticking up over tailgates.

Peter and Jade head off to the Driftwood Diner, while Kimiko and I, and yes, Sabrina, wander in and out of the specialty shops. I decide to buy little presents for everyone back in Cowichan Bay. I buy coffee mugs with an orca on one (for Dad) and a Pacific loon on the other (for Anne). I choose a pair of oven mitts with ravens on them for Nell, two bottle openers in the shape of fish for Ben and Riley, and a book on West Coast seafood cooking for Aunt Maddie. In a funky little bookstore, I find a sketchbook with an eagle printed on the cover for Izzy, and a tiny stuffed otter for her little sister, Amelia. Ramona and Izzy's mom both get handmade wooden knitting needles. Last of all, I snag some surfing decals for Max. No doubt he'll stick them on that old Volvo—the one he seems determined to buy.

All Sabrina buys is a pack of gum at the corner grocery store. She doesn't talk much, and that's fine by me. Kimiko, on the other hand, is like a kid in a candy store. She can't get enough of the little shops. She wants to venture into every single one, and after twenty minutes, I tell her we'll meet her a little later— she is clearly enjoying this long overdue, off-leash time.

"But," I warn her when Sabrina is out of earshot. "Be careful. You're new to this whole human thing. Just don't act too weird, or accept any rides from strangers, or—"

"I won't," Kimiko promises, impatient at having to stand still.

When she disappears into a clothing store, I head off in the opposite direction.

"Where are you going?" Sabrina asks.

"I want to check out the art scene up here."

"The art scene?" she says sarcastically. "Help me control my enthusiasm."

"Well, no one said you had to come, too," I say.

She follows me anyway.

There are tons of galleries peppered along the main street through town. Sabrina mostly looks at the jewellery, but I am mesmerized by the paintings. There's one in particular that catches my eye—a print of Emily Carr's, called "D'Sonoqua: Wild Woman of the Woods." The wooden figure is dark, with hollow sunken eyes and powerful outstretched arms. She is taller than tall, with long matted hair, and the dark, ominous forest looms behind her.

"Apparently the wild woman in the woods used to kidnap children," the woman working in the gallery tells us.

Sabrina puts down the necklace she's been admiring.

"And then she used to eat them," the woman adds.

None of this is news to me. I heard that very same story the summer I was twelve, in Yisella's village. One of the elders told the little kids in the village about her. It was their way of ensuring the kids wouldn't wander into the woods and become lost. I remember how freaked out they were.

I look around to see if Sabrina is listening but she's gone, and then I see her sitting alone on a bench near the post office across the road.

"Well," I tell the woman, "it was nice talking to you."

"You, too," she says cheerily. "Don't go getting lost in the woods, now!"

Hah! If only you knew.

I cross the street and feel compelled to sit beside Sabrina on the bench. She doesn't say anything, just studies her folded hands in her lap. A minute later she starts shredding a gum wrapper into tiny pieces. Something is up.

"Listen," I say, "do you want to get a coffee? Maybe meet up with Peter and Jade at the Driftwood or something?"

She looks at me, her eyes full of tears, and shakes her head, no.

Crap! It's hard watching somebody cry, even when that somebody has sometimes been the reason behind some of your own tears.

"Look, Sabrina. You did your time here," I say. "We're heading home soon."

"Don't you get it?" she wails. "That's the part I hate the most. I mean, I don't want to stay here, but I don't want to go home, either. The only person at home is Rosa, our maid."

"Your parents are still in Hawaii?"

"Correction. My *mother* is still in Hawaii, with Ansell, her Pilates instructor. My dad is somewhere in Oregon. Portland, I think, or maybe Eugene. I really have no idea. Some business trip, as usual."

I don't say anything, because, how is a person supposed to respond to a statement like that?

"Yeah, nice, eh? You remember when my mom called the

other night? Do you know what she said to me?"

I shake my head.

"She said, 'Oh, by the way, Sabrina, your father and I are splitting up. I'm sure you aren't all *that* surprised. But honey, you're going to *love* Ansell. He's likes all the same music you do, plus he has a Porsche!' Can you believe it? And he's like, eleven years younger than my mom, too."

"I'm really sorry, Sabrina."

"It's just that ..."

I wait.

"It's just that you were buying all those little gifts for your family and stuff, and I didn't feel like buying anything for anyone, except Tiffy. How pathetic is my life, eh?" She takes the bit of tissue I offer her and blows her nose with gusto.

"Tiffy counts," I say.

"I know, but you know what I mean. I just ... I just don't want to go back there. I don't want to go back home."

I struggle for the right words, but it's hard. It seems as though the Webber's big beautiful house is pretty empty inside, literally *and* figuratively.

"Come on," I say, taking her arm and hauling her up onto her feet. "You totally need something decadent to eat. I'll even treat."

"Are you insane?" she says, but she still allows me to drag her up the street.

"Probably."

"Wait," Sabrina stops on the sidewalk and looks down at her

shoes. They're fire-engine red, and so *not* Tofino. "I need to say something."

I feel myself stiffen. "Okay."

"It's about what I said the other day? That stuff about your mom."

I chew my bottom lip. "I remember."

"Well, I was just so upset about my parents. I mean, I know that doesn't make it okay or anything, but . . . well, I'm really sorry. It was a really terrible thing to say. Even for me."

I nod my head. "You're right. It was."

"No wonder I don't have any friends. I wouldn't blame you if you never forgave me. You have every reason not to."

I think about that for a minute. "No," I say when we start walking again. "I forgive you." And I'm surprised to find that I do.

I stop outside the door of the Driftwood Diner and fold my arms in front of me. Sabrina raises both her hands in the air in mock surrender. "Okay, okay! You win. Find me something loaded with butter, sugar and nuts."

"That's the spirit!"

"But most important of all?"

"What's that?" I ask.

"Don't cheap out on the chocolate."

Chapter Twenty-Nine

"I CAN'T REMEMBER when I've had a better day," Kimiko says later in the afternoon. We're upstairs in our room, looking over the gifts I bought for everyone. Kimiko picks up the sketchbook and turns it over in her hands.

"This is beautiful." She opens the book runs a hand over the clean white pages. "Is your friend Izzy a good artist?"

"She's amazing," I say truthfully. "She has the coolest job back home. She paints her own designs on kayaks."

"I'd like to visit Cowichan Bay one day," Kimiko says. "Then I can see for myself. And meet your family, too."

I frown, not quite sure of what to say. "You'd like Cowichan Bay, but it looks like I won't be there for much longer."

"You won't? Why not?"

"My father wants to move to Victoria. That's a city about an hour away."

"And you will be separated from each other? How awful!"

"Well," I say, "no. It isn't like that. We'll just be moving to a new house, along with Anne, his girlfriend."

"Oh," Kimiko says, nodding. "And you don't like her?"

"No! Anne is great. It's just that, I like the house we live in now."

"But this is nothing," Kimiko says. "Your home will just be different on the outside. It's the people that matter. You said so yourself."

"I guess I did say that." Why is it so easy to dispense sage advice, yet so hard to take it?

"Well, wherever you end up living, I am going to miss you very much," Kimiko says.

I smile. "But we can keep in touch and stuff. You know about Facebook and Instagram, right?"

Kimiko frowns. "Facebook and Insta-what?"

Wow, becoming "human" when you're already a teenager is going to be a serious challenge, that's for sure.

"I'll explain later," I tell her. Kimiko nods, twisting several of her dark braids thoughtfully in her hand, but there's a crease between her eyebrows that wasn't there a moment ago.

"Relax. It's all going to be fine," I assure her. "You'll see. You just have to take stuff one day at a time."

"Is that another expression?"

"Sort of. It just means don't think too far ahead. Just enjoy the day, you know?"

"I sure hope I don't do anything stupid," she snorts. "I don't ever want to make another mistake."

I laugh. "Hah! Good luck with that."

"Why are you laughing?"

"Because making mistakes is inevitable. It's part of being human. Take it from me, I've got this whole human thing dialed!" Even so, Kimiko doesn't look entirely convinced. Who could blame her? She's building a whole new life.

"So," I say, changing the subject. "Is there a part of the old you that you're going to miss?"

"The old me?"

"You know, your kitsune life. Super X-ray vision at night. Fire starting. Leaping over logs. And what about getting your ninth tail? I mean, that's a major big deal, right?"

"Yes," Kimiko says. "Receiving your ninth tail and the white fur that comes with it is . . . I mean, *was*, the ultimate power, but I'm sure I would have messed it up anyway. And besides, I would have had help to get it, the same way I got my other tails."

"I'm not so sure about that."

"Why do you think that?"

"Because of what you did for Jack," I say. "With the last of your *hoshi no tama*'s power when you smashed it. You sacrificed everything to save him even though you didn't know if you would live or die. Think about that Zenko oath, Kimiko.

What you did was the ultimate benevolent act, and I think it was recognized."

I wait for Kimiko to say something, but she doesn't.

"Think about it!" I do on. "You broke your *hoshi no tama* and lost your kitsune status. So instead of your fox fur turning white, Jack's *feathers* turned white. I think it may have been Inari's way of recognizing your gift."

Kimiko looks thoughtful. "Well, that could be true. I mean, there's not much known about half-kitsunes. Maybe this *is* what happened!"

"And instead of dying, you were given a mortal life! Maybe that is your reward for saving Jack."

Kimiko nods. "That could be, but still . . ."

"Still?"

"I don't know where to start, and I have to admit, I feel a little lost. I don't want to have to depend on others to get by anymore."

"Well, sometimes you have to," I say. "No matter how strong you are, everyone needs a little help now and then."

She doesn't disagree with me, but she doesn't look reassured, either.

"It will all work out, Kimiko. You'll see."

She claps her hands in front of her. "I won't worry about that today," she says, "and can I share something with you?"

"Sure!"

"It's my birthday tomorrow."

"Seriously?"

"Yes, for real. I look pretty good for a nine-hundred-year-old, don't you think?"

"That's crazy!"

"But now it's different," Kimiko says with a contented sigh. "Now I will grow older with each birthday, just like you. So tomorrow, I will be eighteen. That is the age I have chosen. A teenager, but old enough to be on my own."

I have a sudden flash of insight; the perfect birthday gift for Kimiko. I wring my hands together with excitement. This is going to be good.

❈

"Hey, Sabrina?" I say after dinner. "Kimiko and I kind of need your help."

Sabrina is lying on the couch, flipping mindlessly through a fashion magazine. "Sorry," she says, sounding bored. "Busy reading."

I snatch the magazine out of her hands and hold it high over her head. "No, you aren't. And anyway, this is mindless trash."

"But I enjoy mindless trash."

"Well, I guarantee you're going to enjoy this even more."

She sighs, sits up and flops her head against the back of the couch dramatically. "Highly doubtful. What do I have to do?"

"Well," I say, "we need you to be our beauty consultant." This piques her interest, but she looks at me dubiously. "Come on, Hannah. Since when are you interested in anybody's beauty advice?"

"I didn't say it was for me."

"Who, then?"

I tilt my head toward Kimiko, and then extend my hand to Sabrina. When she takes it, I pull her to her feet. "Get off your butt. We're going upstairs."

꧁꧂

Sabrina and I both agree that Kimiko isn't allowed to look in the mirror until we've finished. It's going to be a time-consuming process, and she's not very good at being patient— another human quality she's going to need to learn. It takes a while to undo all of her braids and then we have to comb the snarls out of her long hair.

"Ouch!" she whines when Sabrina fights with a particularly nasty tangle.

"Well, honestly," Sabrina says. "I'm not doing it on purpose. I'm trying to be as gentle as I can. You should take better care of your hair."

When all of Kimiko's braids are finally combed out, we divide it into nine equal sections. Then we pin all but one of them on the top of her head.

"Are you sure this is going to work?" I whisper to Sabrina.

"Positive," she says. "I did it to my cousin last summer."

"Okay, then. Full steam ahead."

Sabrina adds the hydrogen peroxide to the paper cup full of hair conditioner and mixes it thoroughly. Then she digs around in her cosmetic bag and pulls out a soft make-up brush. "This thing cost over twenty bucks," she says. "But I'm sacrificing it in the name of beauty. You can thank me later."

"Very noble of you, Webber," I say, smiling.

"I know."

I'm not going to lie; I have to marvel at Sabrina's talent. She really knows hair, and I watch as she applies the sticky paste quickly and confidently to a section of Kimiko's hair.

"How long do we have to wait?" I ask.

"Patience is a virtue, Hannah," Sabrina says, sounding a lot like a parent.

"I take it that means a long time?" Kimiko slumps her shoulders and groans. "I'm so bad at waiting!" she sulks.

"We noticed," Sabrina and I say in unison.

What Sabrina doesn't say, however, is that we have to repeat the sticky-stuff-on-the-hair process several times, waiting for what seems like forever between the applications.

When we send Kimiko to the shower for her last rinse and shampoo, she high fives both of us with great enthusiasm. We listen to her hum mindlessly as she showers, and literally twiddle our thumbs on our laps as we wait. Finally, the water shuts off.

When Kimiko emerges in a robe with her hair wrapped in a towel, we sit her down away from the mirror, untwist the towel, and once again set about the challenging task of combing out all that hair. Our efforts have been rewarded! The bright white streak down one side of her hair is positively brilliant! It's exactly as I'd imagined it would be!

"Oh my God, Sabrina!" I say. "You're a genius! It looks awesome!"

"Of course it does," she says calmly. "Were you actually worried?"

"Not really," I lie. "I knew you'd pull it off."

I want to hurry along the process, but Sabrina snatches the blow dryer out of my hand, insisting that Kimiko's hair is in need of some "treatment" before it is subjected to the blow dryer. "Attention," I discover, involves a de-frizzing spritzer and something made from tropical plants that grow on the other side of the world. Man, this is more complicated than I thought it would be. Who knew?

"Is all this really necessary?" I say, flopping down on my back on the bed.

"Absolutely," Sabrina says. "You might want to take notes."

I ignore her, but when she finally turns on the blow dryer, I'm fully back in the game.

"Okay," Sabrina says. "She's done. You can do that weird braid thing now if you want."

"Awesome!" I eagerly settle myself on the stool beside a fidgeting Kimiko and pick up the brush.

"I still don't really get it," Sabrina says. "But I guess style is a personal thing. Can I go back to my magazine now?"

"Your work here is done," I say. "You are a free woman. And Sabrina?"

"Yeah?"

"Thanks. This was actually really cool of you."

"Whatever." Sabrina fluffs up her own hair, reapplies her lip gloss, and goes back downstairs.

"Keep your eyes closed," I tell Kimiko, and she obeys, albeit with a lot of fidgeting. I work quickly and carefully, creating four perfect braids on either side of Kimiko's head, securing each one with a bright red elastic band. When I'm finished, I pick up the final section of bleached hair and start on Kimiko's ninth and final braid.

When I'm done, I take hold of her shoulders and propel her toward the big mirror in the bathroom, ordering her to keep her eyes closed. "Okay," I say. "Happy Birthday. You can open your eyes now."

Kimiko stares at her reflection with awe. She picks up the snow-white braid in her hand and her jaw hangs open.

"Well? What do you think?"

"I love it!" she squeaks.

"You didn't get to receive your ninth tail, so I've given you a ninth braid instead."

She doesn't say anything right away. She doesn't have to. Her face says it all. When she brushes the side of her cheek with the tip of the snow-white braid, she looks at me with a big grin on her face. "Thank you, Hannah. This is the best gift ever."

I grab my phone from beside my bed and then pull Kimiko over to stand beside me. "Selfie time!" I snap off a bunch of pictures, most of which are anything but flattering because we're both laughing so hard.

"Look," Kimiko says as we scroll through them. "There I am. There I am, right next to you."

It's so weird that she's never seen a photograph of herself before this moment. "Yep," I say. "There you are, and I have to say, *you* . . . are a total fox!"

Chapter Thirty

꧁꧂

THE YOUNG WOLF WAKES *often during the night. She gets up from the base of the tree where she has bedded down, turns several circles, and curls up again. She licks at her hind paw, healed now, but still tender.*

She is half asleep when she hears the pack. Her ears prick and she sits up, trying to catch its scent high in the air. She stares up at the sky. It will soon be dawn; it will soon be time.

She gets up and pokes her muzzle through the bushes, taking careful steps toward the ocean through the thick forest, until she finds herself on the beach. She takes her weight off her injured paw, and bends down to lick the side of it. It is healing, and perhaps once she is in the water, the discomfort will ease even more.

Soon . . .

She travels along the tops of the logs, through beach grass, over rocks and broken shells, until she sees the house sitting in darkness on the point. No lights. It is still too early. She pads closer, and then closer still, until she is directly beneath the room—the one she knows they share. She sits down and waits, her ears pricked and eyes alert. There has been a change here. A good one—she can sense it. Now she knows the time has come for her to go home.

As though on cue, the pack howls from over the water, from a distant island. At once, the young wolf stands, the tenderness in her paw giving her pause. But she begins the trek back up the beach, confident that she will reach the right spot before dawn breaks.

❧

I wake from a dream about Sitka and rush to the window, bumping straight into Kimiko, who is doing the same thing.

"A dream," she says. "I had a dream. About the Okami."

"You did? So did I!"

"She was sitting right there," she points. "Right outside our window in the dark. Then she went up the beach."

"I had the same dream! The other wolves called to her and she went to them!"

I open the balcony door quietly, grab a couple of the folded blankets from the top of the trunk at the foot of my bed, and hand one to Kimiko. We wrap them around our shoulders and slip outside.

Almost immediately, Jack is on the railing. His splendid white feathers are stark against the still dark sky, and his blue eyes are wide and alert. He is full of frenetic energy, and pecks at the blanket on my arm, pulling at the threads and chortling in raven speak at the same time.

"What is it, Jack?" I say.

He beats his ivory wings furiously, jumps to my shoulder, tugs at a strand of my hair, and then takes off to the shore-line. He circles twice over the water, lets out an ear-splitting cry and heads north, soaring fast just a few feet above the surface of the water.

"We have to go," I say suddenly. "We have to follow him."

"But where to?" Kimiko asks.

"Tofino."

"But, how do you know he's going there?"

"I just do."

We both get dressed quickly and quietly, and then creep down the stairs in stealth mode. Norman opens one eye as we pass by, but doesn't make a fuss.

Once outside, I grab Kimiko's hand and head for the trail that runs down the side of the lodge. "Come on!"

"What now?"

"That little aluminum boat of Ruth's," I say. "The one high up near the dune grass. The water is calm and it's light enough to see!"

"But I've never even been in a boat like that!"

"Well, I was practically born in one," I say, "and Ruth did say I could use it."

We drag the eight-foot skiff over the wet sand and down to the water. It's heavy, but we manage it without losing too much time. The water is freezing, but I sure don't have cold feet!

When we're in the boat, I set the oars in the oarlocks and row with all my might along the shoreline until we're around the point. Then I drop hold of the oars and grab the outboard's pull start. Thankfully, it starts up on the third try.

Kimiko is fidgeting, and I tell her to relax and settle herself in the middle of the boat.

In seconds, we are cutting across the flat surface of the water, and out of nowhere, Jack appears just feet from the boat. He swoops and zigzags in front of us. I know he wants us to follow him, so that's what we do.

"What's he doing?" Kimiko asks.

"He's giving us an escort," I say.

Thank you, Jack. I knew you'd have our backs.

We reach Tofino quickly, and motor past the harbour for a few minutes until we find ourselves in a tiny, heavily forested cove. It's here that Jack banks right and flies to the pebbled shore to light on a piece of driftwood.

I ease up on the throttle and guide the skiff toward the dark wall of trees in front of us. That's when I see her on the beach.

"Look!" Kimiko whispers.

"I know!" I whisper back, cutting the motor. "I see her!"

Sitka is standing at the water's edge, alert ears twitching back and forth.

I tie the boat to a long-abandoned dock at the far edge of the cove.

"What do we do now?" Kimiko asks.

"We wait," I say, "and make sure she crosses safely."

"To that island?"

"Yes," I say. "Meares Island. That's where her pack is. I'm sure of it."

"But what if she can't make the trip? What about her paw?"

"Too many what ifs," I say, even though I'm thinking the same thing.

"So we wait?"

I nod.

And that's exactly what we do; we stop talking and start watching. We wait beneath the pale morning light that spills over the surface of the water.

❦

Sitka paces up and down the shore. She looks out to sea, her stance firm, her silver sweep of a tail held out straight behind her.

That's when the wolf songs start. It rides across the channel—a chorus that floats over the water, through the morning mist, and to Sitka on the shoreline. My goosebumps have goosebumps, and I nudge Kimiko with my elbow. She nods at me, and we hold our breath and watch Jack, still as a statue, as he watches Sitka.

She licks her lips and, excited, paces up and down the beach at the water's edge. Then, she throws her head back and howls, a long, drawn-out, spine-chilling sound that moves all the way down my spine and makes me shiver. Then she walks straight into the water and begins to swim, her ears back behind her and her silver-grey back just above the surface of the water. She paddles in a straight line, putting distance behind her, and I swear she turns and looks right at us as she passes by, only a hundred feet or so from our boat.

"You can do it," I whisper to her. "Jack will be with you."

And he is! He flies in slow circles over her head, then zig-zags back and forth in her path, clearly keeping his eye on her. We watch for a long time until both of them are mere specks against the green water. A little bit later, they are gone altogether.

I pull the cord and start the engine again, but instead of turning for home, I follow in Sitka's wake. I'm not going back until I know she has made the crossing safely. I know we'll catch it from the others back at the lodge, but I'm prepared to take the heat.

We head for Meares Island, and experience a little bit of a chop five minutes out. Kimiko, sitting near the bow, clutches the sides of the boat with both hands while I hold the rudder steady.

I spot Sitka at the same moment that Jack begins to shriek! We see him fly up and down above her, then swoop down close to her head, all the while making the most awful noise!

"What's wrong?" Kimiko shouts over the motor.

I twist the throttle and the boat shoots forward, the bow rising out of the ocean before slapping down hard on the water's surface. In mere seconds, I can see Sitka's head, but the water has covered most of it, and her back is no longer visible at all. There is a lot of splashing, but she's not moving forward. It's plain to see that she is in some kind of trouble!

"She's going to sink!" Kimiko says, panic in her voice.

I ease up on the throttle and pull in beside her, then cut the engine. "Not if I can help it!" I shout. "Here!" I hand Kimiko an oar and tell her to steady the boat as best she can, all the while keeping my eyes on Sitka.

The wolf struggles, her front legs churning the water in front of her, but she isn't paddling fast enough; her hindquarters have dropped far below the surface so that her body is almost vertical in the water. It must be her injured leg. She's exhausted!

"Easy, easy," I say calmly. "You're almost there."

It's true, but Sitka doesn't look as though she could make it ten feet, let alone the 150 it will take to reach the shoreline of Meares Island.

I am desperate—we have to do something! She's so close! She has survived the woods on her own; she has watched over Kimiko; she has stayed alive, despite being hungry, and she is almost home! And whether or not Sitka is Kimiko's Okami guardian wolf, or my spirit animal, she is a wild animal that needs our help. Wolf medicine may be strong, but this creature in front of us isn't invincible.

"She's going to drown, Hannah!" Kimiko says, extending an arm to the flailing wolf. "Help!" When I see the terror on her face, I understand. Water. Drowning. All over again! That fateful day in Honshu, Japan—the day that Kimiko survived, but so many others did not.

Jack lands on the side of the boat, squawking and croaking non-stop to Sitka. I grab hold of the other oar, ensure it's locked in tight, then extend its tip over the side of the boat until the edge of it is level on the water in front of Sitka.

Please! Come on! Come on! Come on!

Sitka's eyes lock with mine and for a brief moment she stops struggling altogether. Just when I'm sure she's going to go under for the last time, she gathers her strength and snaps her jaws onto the side of the oar.

She has to hang on. She just has to!

Her front legs break through the water and begin paddling again, and I don't waste any time. I twist the throttle and ease the boat forward slowly, while Kimiko keeps a tight hold on the oar.

I scan the shoreline of Meares, but I don't see any signs of Sitka's pack. If they would only appear! It would help her to hang on!

We putter slowly toward the gravelly beach, and when we are only twenty feet from the shore, I cut the motor and Sitka's strong jaw finally release the oar. With a sudden burst of energy, her back rises up out of the water and she swims the remaining few metres to the shore.

Kimiko and I hold our breath as Sitka steps out of the water and shakes her coat violently on the shore.

There is no sign of life on the beach, but the little half-grown wolf seems to know where to go. She limps up to the trees, but turns and watches us for a few moments before slinking into the shadows of the big trees.

"Remember what you said to me a while ago?" Kimiko says after Sitka has vanished. She doesn't wait for me to answer her. "You said, 'No matter how strong you are, everyone needs a little help now and then.'"

Before I can respond, Jack flaps his white wings and follows Sitka into the early morning shadows of Meares Island.

Chapter Thirty-One

AS EXPECTED, KIMIKO and I are not in anyone's good books when we get back. In fact, Ruth, Peter, Jade and Sabrina are all waiting on the beach when we come around the point in the skiff. We can see their breath hanging in cold, early morning air.

"Uh oh," I say under my breath, my teeth chattering. "We're in for it now."

While we drag the boat up to the dune grass at the top of the beach, I tell Ruth I wanted to take Kimiko for a little dawn boat ride before we went on our separate ways. After all, who knows when we'll see each other again? But Ruth is clearly disappointed, which makes me feel pretty awful.

"You could have had an accident out there!" she scolds.

"But I've been driving boats since I was six," I say. "And you did say I could use it while I was here, right?"

"Common sense, girl," Ruth says. "Always let someone know where you're going when you're out on the water. Surely you know that rule."

"You're right, Ruth," I say. "I'm sorry."

"Guess he's in the doghouse, too," Peter says, pointing. We all look up to see Jack gliding high over the water on silent wings toward the shore. He perches on the top of a fir tree and nods his head at me in a way that only I understand. I'm *so* glad to see him back so soon, and right away I feel as though a huge weight has fallen from my shoulders, because, I know Jack; there's no way he would leave Meares Island unless Sitka was absolutely safe. Of that I'm sure.

Despite the chill in the air, and the cold reception we received from the others, thinking about Sitka's reunion with her family makes me feel warm inside.

She's back where she belongs.

⁂

By the time mid morning arrives, we've been forgiven. Sabrina, Kimiko and I share out some trail mix, while we watch Jack dive-bomb the beach along with two other ravens.

"He sort of makes the others look bad," Sabrina says. "He's like, the good-looking one in the crowd. I sure know what *that* feels like."

I roll my eyes. Some things never change, I guess. "He's not so much good-looking," I say, "as different."

"Well, whatever. He's got style," Sabrina says. "But I bet those resident ravens will be glad to see us leave."

"I wish you didn't have to," Kimiko says quietly. "Leave, I mean."

"But at least we're all together today," I say.

"What's so special about today?" Sabrina says. "Other than it was pretty awesome to see you get busted by Ruth."

I ignore the comment. "It's Kimiko's birthday."

"It's true," Kimiko says proudly. "I'm eighteen today."

"Eighteen," Sabrina says wistfully. "I'm *so* jealous. If I were eighteen I could just move out and never have to see . . ." Her voice trails off.

"See what?" Kimiko asks.

"Never mind," Sabrina says. "I just wish I was eighteen, that's all. I'd be officially an adult, and no one could tell me what to do. I'd take off. I'd be free as a bird."

That's probably true. The Webbers are pretty loaded. Sabrina is probably financially set for life.

But Kimiko looks worried. "But why would you want to take off? What about your family?"

"They may be my family," Sabrina says, "but they don't *know* me at all. They don't even try."

"That is difficult to understand," Kimiko says. "I am so sorry."

"Why?" Sabrina says. "It's not your fault."

"I know," Kimiko says. "But I'm sad you're unhappy, that's all."

I smile. Kimiko doesn't know it yet, but she's actually pretty good at this "being human" stuff.

"Well, what are *you* going to do?" Sabrina asks her. "Now that you're eighteen, I mean?"

"I don't really know."

"Well, take my advice. Don't stay *here* too long," Sabrina says dramatically. "This place is where fun goes to die."

❦

"What *are* you going to do," I ask Kimiko later on after dinner. "I mean, you can't really stay here forever, right?"

We're lying on a pile of pillows in the Big Kahuna, a bowl of buttered popcorn in front of us, compliments of Ruth, who appears to have forgiven our selfish move of this morning.

Kimiko is beaming, smiling as though she has some kind of news that she's just dying to share.

"I've been giving it a lot of thought," she says. "And doing a lot of research. Ruth helped me at lunchtime, and Jade, too. On the computer."

"Research?" I ask. "What kind of research?" I stuff too much popcorn into my mouth and wipe away some butter from my chin. Why is it impossible to eat popcorn in a dainty fashion? I've tried. It can't be done.

"Well," Kimiko says, sitting up and wiping her buttery hands on a piece of paper towel she tears off from a roll beside us. "I've been thinking a lot about the things you have told me, about your friends back in Cowichan Bay. All the stuff you tell me about your home."

There's that word again. I bite my tongue because, right now, I'm supposed to be the listener.

"Anyway," Kimiko says, "I'm starting a brand new life. Everything will be different now, and I can create my own family for myself. What was that expression you told me the other day?"

"Which one?"

"Something about homes and hearts?"

"Oh. Right. *Home is where the heart is.*" It sounds so cheesy when I say it, and a part of me feels guilty because, truth be told, I'm still not sure if I one hundred percent believe it myself.

"Yes! That's the one."

Her amber eyes light up, and her face glows almost the way it did when she first arrived here. But now it isn't the *hoshi no tama* that gives her so much energy; it's genuine excitement for her future.

"So," she says, clutching her hands together in her lap. "I've decided to go back."

"Back?"

"To Japan."

"You are? Really?"

"Yes, back to Honshu. There are *so* many kids there. Kids

like me, only much younger. Kids who are alone now, who no longer have families."

The orphanages. I've read about them, about how so many children lost their parents in the tsunami and are still without real homes, even years later.

"Jade has done a lot of aid work. She knows of all sorts of organizations who help children like this. She helped me send some emails earlier today."

"So, you want to work with the kids?" I ask.

Kimiko digs into her pocket and pulls out a piece of paper. She unfolds it and hands it to me.

It's a photograph of a large brick building surrounded by tall trees, a hill rising up behind it. There are some Japanese characters written underneath the picture, but of course, none of that means anything to me.

"What is this place?" I ask.

"It was once a school, but now it's become home to a lot of lost children. Most are very young, under six." There is a certain softness in Kimiko's eyes as she stares at the photo in my hands. "I want to go there," she says quietly. "To this very place. I want to help."

"Really? That's so cool, Kimiko!" I say.

"We have already received an email from them, too. They seem very interested. And because I can speak English so well, they say I could really be of some help to them." She looks over her shoulder to ensure we won't be overheard, and then leans in to whisper. "The Okami was watching over me.

I think she was waiting until my transformation was complete. And when it was, she revealed her message."

"Which was?"

"It's all so clear now. She was telling me, that despite everything, I could go back home, with a little help from my true friends, of course." Her face shines.

"Kimiko," I say, a catch in my voice. "I think you're right! And helping out in Honshu is such a great idea."

"I am to wait for an email from a Mr. Nakagawa," Kimiko says excitedly. "They said he would contact me tomorrow, first thing. But Hannah! It sounds as though I will be able to go right away! I mean, if Mr. Nakagawa says it's okay."

"It sure does sound promising," Ruth says, coming in from the kitchen, her hands thrust in her sweater pockets. "If your parents were alive, Kimiko, I'm sure they would be so very proud of you."

Kimiko looks at me and ever so slightly raises an eyebrow. She's obviously told Ruth a different version of her complicated past.

Sabrina comes through the door, rushes past Ruth and begins switching off all the lights in the room.

"Hey!" I say. "What are you doing?"

"You'll see," she says, then shouts over her shoulder, "Are you ready, Jade?"

Jade calls out from the kitchen. "Ready!"

The lights go off, and I hear someone strike a match. Seconds later Jade marches into the Big Kahuna with a cake on a tray that's ablaze with candles, eighteen candles, to be exact.

"OH!" Kimiko says, jumping to her feet.

"A birthday simply cannot go by without cake," Ruth announces matter-of-factly. "It's kind of a rule. At least it is around here."

Kimiko's jaw drops open, and she looks at me with questioning eyes. But I raise both hands up in front of me and take a few steps back. "Well, don't look at me," I say. "I never said a word." Which is entirely true, because I wasn't sure if Kimiko wanted the whole world to know about this, her first authentic *human* birthday!

We both look at Sabrina, who does her best to look like none of this is a big deal. "Whatever." She shrugs. "Guilty as charged." But she's wrong. It *is* a big deal! Kimiko rushes at Sabrina, enveloping her in a giant bear hug until Sabrina begs to be released. Ruth is next, then Peter, Jade and finally me. I have to be honest—I'm surprised, and also pretty impressed that Sabrina is the force behind this celebration. Maybe there's hope for her after all. Maybe this is a "year of change" for all of us.

A little while later, Kimiko and I are flaked out on the cushions in the Big Kahuna, stuffed to the max with cake.

"Well," Kimiko says, licking icing off her fingers, "there's one thing I know for sure."

"What's that?" I ask.

"I think I'm a big fan of this birthday stuff."

Chapter Thirty-Two

LEAVING THE ARTFUL ELEPHANT feels weird. I feel as though I've been at the lodge for so much longer than just ten days. Leaving everyone is way harder than I thought it would be, but knowing that Kimiko has a plan of action is comforting.

We're all chatting on the front steps when she pulls me aside. "Hannah, come here," she whispers, hauling me around to the side of the lodge.

"What?"

"I have something for you," she says. She pulls a small gift from a bag, one wrapped in soft green paper and tied with a piece of lace. On the top, is a beautifully folded origami raven made with bright white parchment paper.

"This is so pretty!" I say. "I don't want to open it!"

"Then don't," she says. "Open it when you get back home."

I lift the paper bird off the package, and inspect it from all angles. It's so delicate, so perfect, its folds so crisp and exact. I lean over to hug Kimiko, carefully holding the paper raven up out of harm's way.

"Okay, everyone," Peter says, slamming shut the tailgate of the Chevy. "Time to go. Mike will be waiting down at the harbour."

Kimiko and I try to be stoic, but we both get a little misty. This seems to upset Norman a little, and he tries to worm his way in between us.

We both walk over to the birdbath, where Jack sits perched in all his glory. He has a long flight ahead of him, and eagerly eats the piece of toast with peanut butter I saved for him; energy food, even for birds.

"Don't dawdle," I tell him sternly. "Fly straight home."

Jack flaps his wings and hops onto my shoulder. He tugs my hair, and then in a flash of white, is up in the air and headed south.

Everyone applauds, and Norman barks like a lunatic while he runs in excited circles around the birdbath.

I squeeze into the back seat next to Sabrina. Ruth leans in through the window and pats my arm. "You girls take care of yourselves," she says, "and you make sure you both come back for a visit real soon, you hear?"

"We will," Sabrina and I say at the same time, and for some

reason, even though Sabrina claims to have had a horrible time here, I think she just might.

Peter checks his phone and mutters something about girl-friends who are always late, just as Jade trots down the front steps, her own backpack slung over her shoulder. "Sorry, sorry," she says. "Warren called to say the water taxi is down for a few days. And then he started to talk. You know Warren. He likes to talk!"

"That's an understatement!" Ruth laughs.

"He wouldn't stop talking about the wolves!"

"Wolves?" I am so enthusiastic that I bump my head on the truck's ceiling. "Ouch!"

"Yeah. He saw them from the water taxi yesterday, about six or seven of them, a couple of younger ones, too, one of which had a bit of a lame back leg."

"Or it could be just a Warren story," Ruth says, grinning. "That guy is notorious for telling tales."

"Hmmmm, I don't think so," Jade says thoughtfully. "He said he watched them all playing on the beach, and then they all took to the water and swam toward Miller Channel, up toward Flores Island."

"Won't they get tired?" I pipe from the back seat, thinking about Sitka's leg.

"Nah," Peter says. "Wolves can island-hop all the way up the coast. There are so many of little ones out there."

"I wonder why they didn't stay on Meares," I say.

"Small pack, and they're probably looking for new

territory," Peter says. "It's getting pretty busy around these parts. My bet is they're going to end up at the north end of the island. Just a guess."

Kimiko and I share a secret smile. I'm surprised by the sudden rush of emotion I feel, one that makes me wipe a quickly forming tear from the corner of my eye before anyone can spot it. Everybody seems to be finding their own place, and it feels good.

~❈~

When Peter pulls into the parking lot in the harbour, we see Mike on the dock, vigorously rubbing down the windows of his plane with an old brown towel.

"Well, I guess this is goodbye," Peter says, turning around in the seat. "Gonna miss you girls."

"It's not *really* goodbye," Jade says, smiling. "Peter and I are headed to Vancouver in a couple of weeks, and we'd like to stop in at Cowichan Bay on our way back for a quick visit."

"Seriously? That would be awesome!" I find a crumpled lunch bag on the floor of the truck, tear off a bit and write down my cell number on it.

Peter takes the paper, and then hands it to Sabrina. "Well?"

"You want mine, too?" She flushes, her eyes wide with disbelief.

"Well, of course," Peter says. "I know you have a phone."

Sabrina writes down her number underneath mine, and

beams when Peter folds the paper in half and puts it in his wallet.

"We'll expect the full tour when we see you," Jade says. "The Salty Dog for fish and chips?"

I nod by head. "Absolutely. It can be our first stop."

As we lug our stuff across the parking lot, Peter calls out from the truck. "Hey, Hannah!"

I stop. "Yeah?"

"Look after *yáahl*."

"Pardon me?"

"Yáahl. That's Haida for raven. Look after Jack."

"Oh!" I shout back. "I will!"

It's a given.

⁂

Why does the journey home always seem so much faster that the trip out? It only feels like a few short minutes before we are flying over Cowichan Bay. As Mike lands the Beaver, I study the smattering of boats anchored a little way out on the water. I know each and every one of them: *Faralito*, with her bright yellow cabin; *Persephone*, the wooden sloop with the sky blue headsail; and *Zeelandia*, an old renovated fishing boat that's home to Hans and Selinde, an eccentric Dutch couple.

Behind the boats looms the towering rock face of Mount Tzouhalem. The alders are budding, and are covered with soft green fuzz. It won't be long before the Garry oak meadows up there will be in bloom. It's one of my favourite places to visit in the spring. And it looks as though this spring will be my last around here. A lump forms in my throat but I do my best to push away the invasive thoughts of our impending move to Victoria.

"What's with you?" Sabrina asks from her seat. "You don't look that stoked to be home." She takes a compact mirror out of her bag and starts fussing with her hair.

"I'm just tired," I lie.

As we taxi into the marina, my thoughts turn to Kimiko. I wonder what she is doing this very minute? Maybe she's back on the computer in the Big Kahuna, making her arrangements with the people at the Japanese orphanage. Maybe they've already sent her photos of the children who live there—the kids she will undoubtedly end up playing "big sister" to. Or maybe she's out on the beach thinking about Sitka, remembering the way the wolf stayed close to her until the time was right for her to return to her family.

Mike glides up to the government dock and has the Beaver secured in no time. Sabrina and I scramble out of the plane, and I stretch out my back a little.

"Well," Mike says, "I guess I'll be seeing you a little later on, Hannah. Your aunt has invited me for dinner tonight on your houseboat." I swear he blushes a little when he says this. It's kind of cute—the guy is obviously completely smitten with Aunt Maddie. He clears his throat and helps us with our stuff, then tips his hat to Sabrina. "And I hope you had a good spring break, Katrina."

"Meh," Sabrina says, but she smiles at him, and doesn't give him a hard time about getting her name wrong again either. "Oh, and thanks for the ride."

"My pleasure," Mike says, sounding a little surprised. He's not the only one!

We thank him for everything and say goodbye, and when Sabrina and I get to the bottom of the stairs that lead up to the road, we stop. She's going up them, and I'm hanging a right. For a moment, there is a bit of an awkward silence.

"Well," I say first. "I guess I'll see you at school on Monday."

"Yeah."

"Some spring break, hey?"

"Yeah."

"Is someone coming to pick you up?"

"I'll text Rosa. I'm sure she'll be around."

"You can wait at my place if you want."

"That's okay. I think I'll get a coffee from the Dog. I haven't had a quality dose of caffeine since we left."

"Okay. Well, I'll see you at school, then."

"Sure. See ya."

I watch her climb the stairs, wrestling with her shiny pink suitcase as it bumps up the steps behind her. For some reason I can't seem to walk away.

"Hey!"

She stops on the steps and turns around. "Mmmm?"

"I kind of feel like some tea. Do you want some company?"

She eyes me suspiciously. "Don't you want to watch for Jack or something?"

"Oh. He'll be a little while. He's got a long flight ahead of him, around 165 kilometres. Well, you know, as the crow flies."

"Don't you mean, as the raven flies?"

I laugh. "True."

The tea is delicious, and I can't help thinking how odd it is that I'm sharing a table in the Salty Dog with Sabrina Webber . . . by choice! Truth be told, it isn't even that awful. We talk about school and our favourite movies, and discover we actually have a couple of things in common, at least as far as rating our teachers go. Who knew?

"Refill?" Bea, the co-owner of the Dog asks us. Sabrina looks at me as though she's waiting for me to make the decision.

"Sure," I tell Bea. "Thanks."

An hour later I unlatch the gate next to the Salty Dog, go back down the stairs, and walk over to dock #5. Aunt Maddie is picking my dad up from the airport, and they won't be here until closer to dinnertime. Max is due back from Mexico this afternoon, too, and I've already invited both he and Izzy (*sans* Tyler) to join the rest of us for dinner. But right now, I'm glad to have a little time to myself. I need to prepare for the reactions everyone is going to have to Jack's new look when he shows up. I'm still not sure how I'm going to explain it!

And then, just like that, I see him! A bright white speck perched on top of the lookout on the estuary trail across the water. It's got to be Jack. It's always been his favourite place to perch. He's back so soon? I marvel at the way the afternoon sun glances off his wing, and try not to think about how my life might be without Jack around to share it.

A minute after I set foot on the deck of our houseboat, he arrives. He's none the worse for the wear, just a couple slightly ruffled feathers.

"Whoa! How did you get back here so fast?" I shake my head and hold out my arm. Sure enough, he lights on my shoulder, and I'm comforted by the familiar weight of him. "Welcome home, Jack."

Home. There's that word again.

Chapter Thirty-Three

"PEOPLE ARE GOING to want to know about this," my aunt says. We're all sitting in our living room—Max, Izzy, Mike, Aunt Maddie and my dad—having enjoyed one of my aunt's epic spaghetti dinners.

"She's right, Han," Dad says. "If that really is Jack, you can't expect a radical change like this to go unnoticed."

"Oh, Jack will be noticed all right," I say, "but why does there have to be a logical explanation?"

"Come on," Izzy says. "You know what people are like around here."

"I just don't get it," Max says, slumped on our couch. His normally mousy hair is a shade or two lighter from the sun, and he's got a pretty impressive tan. "I've heard of white ravens before, but to actually change from black to white? No one is *ever* going to buy it."

"But," I say. "You guys believe me, don't you? I mean, you can't deny it. That is most definitely Jack."

We all look out the window at the same time to see Jack walking along the railing with his trademark hip-hop shuffle.

"Of course it's Jack," Aunt Maddie says. She looks to Mike for backup, but he just smiles and shrugs. He's clearly enjoying the conversation.

"I agree," Izzy says. "Without a doubt."

"For sure," Max says.

Dad walks over to the window, his fingers drumming thoughtfully on the side of his face. Jack freezes and stares right back at him. It's a classic Mexican standoff. Then, I swear to God, he sticks out his tongue at my father.

Dad holds his hands in surrender. "Okay! I concede! It's Jack."

❦

"Annie has keys to the new house," Dad says the next morning from the kitchen. "Madds and I were thinking of meeting her down there for another look-see. You up for a road trip, honey?"

I shake my head. I'd rather stick pins in my eyes. "I just got back," I say from the couch. I pick up a magazine—one about wooden boats—and start flipping madly through the pages.

Dad sits down beside me, a cup of coffee in his hand. "Look, I know this is hard for you, Han, but it might help if you actually saw the place."

Flip. Flip. Flip.

"Not interested."

He looks crestfallen, but quickly pastes on a smile and leans over to give my shoulder a squeeze. "Okay, okay. There's no rush. You just have a nice morning. Annie and I will be back a little bit later."

He gets up to search for his wallet, whistling and doing his best to appear cheerful. But the whistle lacks its usual energy and his shoulders are stooped, and I feel worse because he's trying so hard to cover up his oh-so-obvious disappointment.

"Can Izzy and Max come too?" I ask.

Dad finds his wallet on top of the refrigerator, chucks it in the air with one hand and catches it behind his back with the other. "You bet, Hannah Banana. The more, the merrier!"

❧

I don't say a word all the way to Victoria, but no one notices because, as usual, Aunt Maddie yaks non-stop the entire way. But when we turn onto Douglas Street in town, my heart starts pounding and I feel a little sick. Sensing my anxiety, Max takes my hand.

We make a left on Fort Street and then a right onto Cook

Street, destined for the village centre. We pass coffee shops, a second-hand clothing store and a winemaking place. Dad makes turns onto a road with an antiquated Tudor-style book-store on the corner.

"Almost there," he says cheerily.

When we turn down a narrow lane, I immediately spot "Opal," Anne's little white Fiat parked halfway down the street. Dad pulls in behind her and shuts off the engine.

I roll my window down and stare at a little cottage that sits between a heritage house on one side, and a giant maple tree on the other. The cottage is white with black trim, and has a bright red door with a wrought iron knocker in the centre.

"Welcome to number 9 Sitka Lane," Dad says. "Shall we?"

I freeze. "Wait, that's the name of this street?"

"According to the sign on the corner," Dad says, laughing.

I look at the gate in front of the house, and sure enough, a big black number 9 sits right smack in the centre of it.

There's something about the number nine . . .

"Hello? Earth to Hannah? You still with us?" Aunt Maddie teases.

Before I can say anything, Izzy pipes up from the back seat. "Wow. Check that out!" She points to the little turret on the second floor where a diamond-pane, leaded-glass window hangs open. There's a blue birdhouse to one side of it, some grass and twigs protruding from its entrance. Spring has definitely sprung.

The front door opens and Anne emerges. Her dark hair is

tied back with a blue scarf, and she waits on the front step with her arms folded, looking more than a little anxious.

Dad opens his door. "Come on. Everybody out."

I walk up the front path, and Anne pulls me in for a hug. "How was your trip, honey?"

"It was good, thanks," I say.

She keeps an arm draped around my shoulder and steps off to one side as the others rush past. "Hey," she says softly, after they've disappeared inside. "I know this is tough for you."

"Yeah."

"Just have a snoop around, okay? Take all the time you need." She kisses my cheek and walks into the house in search of my dad. I like that she didn't pull the *"you're going to love it here"* stuff. She stops in the hallway and points above her head. "Oh, and the little turret upstairs? It's yours."

"Seriously?" Izzy and Max say at the same time. They both make a beeline for the staircase. I trail up the stairs after them.

The room is small and filled with diffused golden light that filters in from the window. The floors are hardwood, scuffed and marked, but polished to a deep low lustre. I walk over to the window and look out over the road. A little boy is playing with a small brown dog—a dachshund—on the sidewalk. Two houses over, a woman digs in her flower bed. I push open the window and find I can just touch the end of a branch of the big maple. That's one good thing, I guess; Poos and Chuck will appreciate the easy access to the great outdoors.

"Hannah! Look at this!" Izzy and Max are standing next to an open door at the side of the room.

"Closet?" I say.

But it isn't a closet. It's another room—a tiny one with a built-in desk that sits under a window with bright yellow curtains. There is a long, low shelf running the length of the little room, with a custom-made padded cushion on top of it, its fabric printed with colourful cats lounging on stacks of books. When I lift a corner of the cushion, I find a blue, well-chewed squeaky mouse toy hiding underneath it.

"Cats lived here," Max says. "Poos and Chuck will love this room."

"Let's go check out the backyard," Izzy says, already through the door.

Dad, Aunt Maddie and Anne are in the garden, staring up at a gnarled old apple tree that is beginning to show the first hint of pink blossoms. There are five trees in total, and Anne tells us they are all fruit bearing.

"Apple butter, Hannah," she says with shining eyes. "We'll be able to feed the entire neighbourhood." I smile. Man, she's trying so hard.

Along with the fruit trees is a big tangle of wild roses, a fenced vegetable garden, a slightly tilted greenhouse, and . . . a white raven perched on its window ledge! What? My heart lifts, and I can't help but laugh out loud.

Jack squawks at us, but becomes distracted by his reflection in the greenhouse window. I swear he's checking himself out; he even does a little over-the-top preening and strutting.

"Jack!"

He flutters down and lands in the grass at my feet. I extend my arm, but he is way too busy checking the place out to fuss about having a bonding moment with me.

"I think he approves," Max says, grinning.

I press my forehead into his shoulder and close my eyes. "What about you?" I say. "What do you think of this place?"

"I like it, Han. The whole place . . . I dunno, it feels good."

I'm not going to lie; much as I've been resisting, the house *does* feel good. And when we all go into the kitchen after Anne has made tea and warmed up biscuits she bought in Cook Street village, it *smells* good, too.

I take my mug of tea and wander through the living room to the front window. The dachshund and the little boy are still playing on the sidewalk. When he sees me watching them, he stands up and waves. I wave back.

I guess as houses go, number 9 Sitka Lane could be worse.

⚜

When we get back to Cowichan Bay, I clomp up the spiral staircase to my loft, kick off my shoes and flop down on my bed. It's funny—Dad was right—I do feel better after seeing the house, and it was awesome having Max and Izzy and Jack there with me. And the address! How crazy is *that*?

A moment later my phone pings. It's a Facebook notification. I open it to discover a friendship request from someone called "White Fox." A huge smile spreads across my face as I log on and view the profile. And there she is: a pretty face framed by a multitude of dark braids, except for one that stands out from the others—a bright white one!

Talk about fast. Facebook-savvy already! I click on ACCEPT, and right away the space between us doesn't seem as vast.

That's when I remember her gift! How could I have forgotten? I unzip the pocket on my backpack and place the origami raven carefully on the shelf beside all the things Jack has brought me over the years. Then I unwrap the gift. The delicate tissue paper comes off in one piece to reveal a plain flat cardboard box. Inside, is a tiny scroll of parchment paper—the same kind the raven was made from—tied in the middle with a white satin ribbon.

I slip the tassel off the scroll and smooth out the delicate parchment. It's a poem: a haiku poem. The ornate script has been carefully written in fine, black ink, maybe a fountain pen? I read the poem, and then I read it again. It's beautiful. Simple. It's perfect.

I place the paper between the pages of my journal. I want to be able to read it every night before I go to sleep, no matter *where* I live. Because the seventeen syllables Kimiko has written comprise words I don't ever want to forget:

The message was there
In bright white wings & wild woods
Showing me the way.

ABOUT THE AUTHOR

CAROL ANNE SHAW is the author of three novels for young adults, and when she isn't writing, she can often be found at her easel, swinging a paintbrush. "I love writing for kids," Carol Anne says. "They have such an authentic and refreshing way of viewing the world and everything in it. Kids give you the straight answer, they seldom suffer fools, and they know what they like. I respect that."

Hannah & the Wild Woods is the third book in the "Hannah" series. The first novel in the series, *Hannah & the Spindle Whorl*, won a 2011 Silver Medal in the Moonbeam Children's Book Award and was a BOTYA 2010 Finalist in the Young Adult Fiction Category. The second novel, *Hannah & the Salish Sea*, was shortlisted for a 2014/2015 Chocolate Lily Award, and was included in the Canadian Children's Book Centre's Spring 2014 edition of *Best Books for Kids & Teens*. Carol Anne lives with her husband, also an artist, and their beagle, Eddie, in a little house in Cobble Hill on Vancouver Island. Please visit her at her website at www.carolanneshaw.com, on Facebook at facebook.com/carolanneshawauthor, or on Twitter, @CarolAnneShaw.

MARQUIS

Québec, Canada

RECYCLED
Paper made from
recycled material
FSC® C103567

Printed on Enviro 100% post-consumer EcoLogo certified paper,
processed chlorine free and manufactured using biogas energy.